Marriage Under FIRE

Book Four in the Grayce Walters Romantic Suspense Series

plus Bonus Content

A CHRISTMAS WEDDING CEREMONY

JACKI DELECKI

To my wondrous children—
you make my days brighter.

ACKNOWLEDGMENTS

Thank you to my astonishing team of experts. Helen Fitzpatrick, Executive Director of Administration, Seattle Fire Department, Karuna, my plot partner, Faith Freewoman, my amazing editor, and Cynthia Garlough, Romance consultant extraordinaire. And to my support team who keep me writing. Maria Connor, and Jen Rice.

CHAPTER ONE

Maddy Jeffers always chose daring over caution.

With her pelvis thrust forward by her three-inch, knockoff designer heels, she countered her absurd posture by throwing back her shoulders. Since she was on the carpet, she might as well make it a Hollywood red carpet. Placing each foot very firmly and carefully, she managed to avoid teetering and made her way down the silent, sterile hallway of Seattle's Henry Jackson Federal Building. The gunmetal gray walls and the Pine-Sol smell of a moldering, uncaring bureaucracy took her right back to her years as a foster child—in another government building, her future in question again.

Instructed to report out of uniform, she had been in a major quandary. Should she arrive dressed as the ecoterrorist she'd been posing as during her last undercover assignment to make it easier for them to reprimand her? Or should she look like any other office worker?

Major Hunter Hines, her partner on the assignment, had texted her to report at 20:00 to JFB.

The man could have given her a heads-up about what she faced; Marines took care of their own. Of course, Major Hunter Hines wouldn't allow anything like human emotions or the dangers of that particular assignment to affect his report.

Speak of the devil, there was Hunter, waiting in front of the glass door to the FBI office. She surreptitiously dried her sweaty palms on her tight black dress and added a swagger to her slow, agonizing walk. No way would she admit, even under the threat of torture, that her killer shoes were killing her.

His dark, piercing eyes studied her every step. Did she imagine it, or had his Marine posture stiffened and his dark olive skin flushed when he saw her? Perhaps she wouldn't be the only one to suffer today.

Dressed in a dark suit with an open, oxford-blue shirt, long, inky black hair brushing the collar, he looked the part of a billionaire playboy or techie mogul—the cold devil looked mighty good. She tried to ignore the fact that he was sexy as hell and remember he was a pain in the ass.

"What the—" His eyes narrowed, and she waited to hear the censure in his voice. "You don't look like a Marine."

What was a Marine working undercover supposed to look like? And why was it always an issue for a woman, but never a man? He didn't look like a Marine today, either.

The young saleswoman at Macy's told her this was an office dress. How would Maddy know what women wore to their jobs? She had never worked in an office and hoped to God she never would.

Her chin hitched up an inch. She was immune to his snide, unanswerable remarks. "Good morning, sir. My instructions were to report out of uniform." No matter what she wore, she was a Marine, through and through. "I'm blending in."

"Blending in? You call that sexy getup blending in?"

She looked up at him with her best innocent face. "You think it's sexy?"

She pulled at the snug dress riding partway up her thighs.

He watched her movement with his usual eagle eye focus. She didn't miss the hitch in his breath and the way his muscular throat rippled when he swallowed. "Think what?"

Hunter Hines lost for words—she was already feeling better.

"If I'm going to be reprimanded in front of the FBI, I might as well look good."

"Reprimanded? Why would you think you that?"

Because he was a precision machine who did everything by the book. She could envision how he recounted—in painstaking detail—her failure to identify the ecoterrorist who had planned to blow up Seattle's waterfront.

"Didn't you report that it was Sergeant Welby and his dog, Talley, who discovered the bomb?"

"Yes, and I'm glad they did."

If this was one of his tests to prove his power over her, she wouldn't give him any satisfaction. She'd take it square on the chin. She had used attitude to get her through a lot of dicey moments in her past.

"You could've been killed," he continued.

She almost fell off her high heels. She scrutinized his face, looking to see some hint of sarcasm. Hunter almost sounded like he cared. He kept her locked with his intense gaze, as if he wanted all her secrets. She had a shitload, but no one was privy to them.

No one.

"I thought we were meeting with the FBI agents to review the bombing." She wasn't about to reveal her misguided fears about the meeting. Why belabor her screw-up when he was being almost nice.

"My orders came directly from Colonel Dawson. You and I are to report to the FBI office. And, like you, I have no idea what this is about. I thought I was headed back to Camp Pendleton."

He opened the door to the office. "Shall we go in and find out?"

CHAPTER TWO

Hunter held the door open for Maddy. He tried to keep his focus straight ahead like a well-trained Marine, but with a will of their own, his eyes tracked the sleek dress hugging her sweet, rounded ass.

His well-honed training and unshakeable discipline went to hell whenever his sister's best friend was nearby. Maddy Jeffers was more of a challenge than any assignment the Marines had thrown at him. Had the gods in heaven laughed at him when he'd been assigned to work with this tiny blond bombshell?

It would be a relief to return to his normal routine of dangerous, clandestine operations, he reminded himself. Who was he kidding? He'd miss Maddy—the way her eyes brightened in mischief, the way she ran her fingers through the bouncy curls, and the way she lifted her chin when challenged, as if to say to the world, "Give me your worst. I can take it."

A silver-haired woman wearing red-framed glasses low on her nose and a utilitarian suit of navy blue moved around the front desk. "Major Hines? And Second Lieutenant Jeffers?"

Hunter stepped forward and took charge. "Yes, ma'am."

"Lieutenant Colonel Dawson is waiting for you."

"The colonel is here?" Maddy squeaked.

Ignoring Maddy's surprised response, the woman pushed her glasses back up her nose and addressed Hunter. "He and the agents will see you now."

Maddy raised her eyebrows at him as if he had answers. The colonel must have reviewed the report by now. Surely there was nothing in it to warrant a visit to Seattle.

"Follow me, please." The secretary wore low-heeled shoes, unlike Maddy, who wobbled along in high heels, probably trying to add to her five-foot stature.

Maddy toyed with her lively curls—a nervous habit he found endearing.

He walked behind the two women, but this time he focused straight ahead. He hated the unexpected. His survival depended on his ability to assess and control a situation. The arrival of his commander was unforeseen and out of his control.

Hunter watched Maddy as she donned her Marine armor—spine straight, chin up, eyes forward. If it weren't such a turn-on, he'd laugh at the combination of her Marine stance with the hot dress and heels.

"Sir." He and Maddy saluted their commander.

The colonel was in his late fifties, a career Marine who had a tough, take-no-prisoners presence with his clipped, military-grade haircut and ramrod posture. The humorless officer was seated at the end of a black veneer table. There was no mistaking what he expected from his subordinates.

"At ease, Nugget." The colonel smiled at Maddy after using the military slang for rank of Second Lieutenant.

"Yes, sir." Maddy stood down but didn't relax her military bearing.

Hunter jerked his head when the colonel spoke. "Hines, good work by you and Jeffers in apprehending the suspect." The colonel smiled at Maddy again—a shocking response Hunter had never before witnessed from his commander. He'd have bet his father's KA-BAR knife that the colonel would hold to the old school belief that women couldn't be Marines. But just like him, the colonel had fallen under the spell of this petite, kick-ass Marine. It was obvious the commander liked Maddy's clear dedication and self-confidence.

"Thank you, sir," Hunter and Maddy replied together.

The colonel turned and spoke to two younger men straight out of *Men in Black* with their dark suits, white shirts, dark ties, and black, regulation shoes. Which agency were they from— FBI, NSA, or Homeland Security? They all dressed the same. Then Hunter recognized one of the two men as Tim Darney, an FBI agent.

Hunter gave him a slight nod of recognition.

The colonel's forceful voice jolted Hunter back to attention. "You're both familiar with Darney from your debriefing. This is Ron Forret, who sits on the National Joint Terrorism Task Force. He's the reason we're here."

So Ron Forret wasn't FBI; most likely, he was Homeland Security.

"Shall we sit down and get to it? I've got one hour before my next meeting." The colonel didn't waste time on further niceties.

Both men had stood when he and Maddy entered the room. Darney headed right to Maddy. Hunter recognized a man in pursuit, and it wasn't FBI business he was chasing. The fine hairs on the back of Hunter's neck stood on end. He immediately went into possessive mode and started toward Maddy, but checked himself. She wasn't his to protect any longer. Their mission was over.

Maddy smiled at the young man, the smile Hunter wanted to be his alone.

The colonel pointed to the chair next to him. Hunter seated himself several chairs down from Maddy and Darney.

The colonel turned to Forret. "Why don't you bring them up to speed?"

Remote in hand, Forret stood in front of a large screen. He looked back and forth between Maddy and Hunter. "We've been searching through our bomber's devices, communications, and connections. It turns out Brandon Billow isn't simply a crazy, working through his mommy issues. We found a passport and airline ticket for him to Jakarta. We also found a connection to this terrorist group on his computer."

Forret pushed a button, and a PowerPoint image appeared on the screen. Forret read aloud the information from the slide. "Jemaah Islamiyah, meaning 'Islamic Congregation,' frequently abbreviated JI, is a Southeast Asian militant Islamist terrorist organization. Since the start of the U.S.-led war on terror, it has shifted its attention to targeting U.S. and western interests in Indonesia and the broader Southeast Asian region. This group has links to both the Taliban and Al-Qaeda, and, now we believe, ISIS."

The colonel interrupted the presentation to look at Maddy. "Did Billow give any clues as to his association with this group?"

Maddy blushed a rosy pink. "No, sir. And, as you know from the report, I didn't recognize Billow as the bomber."

Hunter hated the way Maddy threw herself on her sword, but at the same time, he admired her for her honesty. She felt guilty because she hadn't read the sociopath correctly. Psychologists and trained profilers missed sociopaths. She was too darn hard on herself.

He'd like to help her lighten up, although she'd laugh herself silly at that idea. She saw him as a boring old man.

Hunter interrupted Maddy's confession. "I thought the Indonesians took out the group's leadership after the Bali bombing in 2006."

Forret turned to Hunter. "You're right, Major. This group had lost its momentum, but we're getting some chatter about the beaten down militants aligning themselves with ISIS. Like weeds, you can never keep these fanatic groups from poking back up."

Hunter tried to grasp the implications of Forret's presentation. "There is an active Jemaah Islamiyah cell with connections to ISIS in Seattle, and that crazy Brandon Billow was part of the cell?"

"We don't know. That's what we're trying to discover. We only have the one name. We don't know if Brandon Billow was recruited, and so far, he refuses to answer. He's trying to cop a plea and won't tell us anything."

Maddy leaned forward. "I have trouble believing Brandon was accepted by a terrorist organization. He was on the fringe of the ecoterrorist group. He's a loner, a 'hanger-on.'"

"All we have is that he made a connection with a person of interest and he was getting ready to travel to Jakarta. He might have been recruited specifically for a mission in Jakarta. We're not sure if he was to play a role, but these groups are very good at enlisting the disenfranchised."

Hunter cleared his throat. "But he was an ecoterrorist, not an angry Muslim. Why would he associate with JI? Or ISIS? They're not exactly guardians of the environment."

Forret nodded. "He doesn't exactly fit the profile. But who ever does? The psychologist who evaluated him said he's obsessed with American corporations and the men who run them. The psychologist believes Billow's behavior was a way to strike out against his father because Billow felt powerless against his abuse."

"Could make him a perfect candidate to strike out against American companies," Darney added.

"But I thought he targeted Dr. Walters because she reminded him of his mother," Maddy said.

Forret shook his head and straightened his tie. "Let's just say he has big issues with both parents. Billow was originally obsessed with you, Lieutenant Jeffers. If you had played his game, he would've acted much more quickly on his plan, and we all know what the outcome would've been. It was very fortunate that his identification with Dr. Walters swayed him away from his sexual fixation with you."

"What the hell does that mean?" Hunter asked. Maddy had been living with a sociopath who had become obsessed with her, and she didn't report it?

"If Billow hadn't been distracted by Dr. Walters, he might have acted on his violent fantasies to blow up Pier 69 sooner in order to prove himself to Lieutenant Jeffers."

The colonel leaned back in his chair and looked at Maddy. "You did good work, keeping that lunatic from acting."

"Thank you, sir." Maddy kept her eyes down and shifted in her seat.

"Forret, get to the point of why you need my Marines," the colonel directed.

"The man Billow made contact with has been on our radar. He has made several trips to Jakarta where his ill uncle now lives. He and his father both served with the Afghan National Army against the Taliban. When his father was killed, he and his family immigrated to the U.S."

Forret showed a picture of a young man in his mid-thirties with dark eyes and a beard. "This is Abu Abdul Hamman. He lives in an apartment complex in the Rainier Valley with his sister and mother. He owns a restaurant close to his home called Afghan Kebab."

Hunter shook his head. "He served with the ANA. Why the change in political allegiance?"

"We believe that his father's death by an American drone radicalized him, and that Abu Abdul Hamman is the link between JI and ISIS in Seattle. The Task Force didn't have any solid leads until this connection with Billow. The man is squeaky clean."

The colonel sat forward and watched Maddy. "Jeffers, we need your help."

Maddy sat up straight in her chair. "Yes, sir. Whatever is necessary."

Hunter's insides thumped with fear. Maddy was totally competent, but she had just come off assignment and was supposed to be on medical leave for her PTSD—not that she'd ever admit to needing help.

The colonel nodded to Forret and the man continued. "We

want you to do the work you were trained to do in Afghanistan. We will place you at the Women's Refugee Center, where Abu's sister and mother attend English classes with other women. With your knowledge of both Pashto and Dari languages, you'll be able to infiltrate their world, gain their trust, and get us access to the brother."

Maddy beamed. Her blue eyes sparkled, and she was grinning while Hunter's gut churned with emotions he refused to acknowledge. He had known this was the end of his work with Maddy, but the new assignment sounded too risky. In Afghanistan, Maddy engaged with the women to gather intel, but there had been a whole platoon of Marines to keep her safe. Who was going to keep her safe in Seattle? Darney, with his freckles and round, cherubic face, who barely looked twelve years old?

"Your cover is that you have recently returned from working with the International Committee of the Red Cross," Forret continued.

"Yes, sir."

Hunter sat back in his chair, pretending a nonchalance he in no way felt, and waited for the colonel to assign Maddy to work in the field with Darney.

The colonel turned abruptly in his swivel chair. "Hines, I want you on this assignment, too."

The roar of Hunter's pounding heartbeat thundered in his ears. Heaven and hell all mixed together.

"Based on your high praise of Jeffers on the last assignment, it's obvious you work well together."

Hunter saw Maddy's head jerk up. Did she really believe he was such an ass that he'd criticize her performance? Guess so, by the way her mouth slackened and she tilted her head and stared at him.

He suddenly noticed the silence in the room while everyone watched and waited.

The colonel kept looking between him and Maddy. "Is there a problem, Hines?"

As if he had a choice. "No, sir."

"Good. Forret, tell them what you've set up."

"We've rented a house on the same street as the apartment complex where the Hamman family lives. You'll monitor their activities from the house. We're not sure of risk, but we're taking this assignment very seriously, Jeffers. Hines will be doing surveillance and will be your backup. This is a joint operation with everyone known to God as part of the team. The idea of ISIS in Seattle has every agency on high alert."

Maddy leaned forward on her elbows, intent on the details of their mission, while Forret continued. "You'll work at the center. Hines will pose as your engineer husband who worked on the clean water project for the ICRC while you helped reunite displaced families from the war."

Hunter felt a kick to the solar plexus. He was going to have to live with Maddy as her husband? The gods were really messing with him. It would take all his years of discipline to keep his hands off her.

Maddy's gasp was loud of enough for everyone to hear. "I have to…I have to pretend Hunter is my husband?" Confident Maddy seemed to have trouble breathing as she sputtered and took several deep breaths. You'd think the colonel was sending her into the deep caves of Afghanistan.

The colonel spoke in his hard-hitting, clipped voice that made probies shake in their boots. Maddy, not recognizing the threat, or simply not intimidated, drummed her fingers in staccato rhythm on the table.

"Is there a problem, Jeffers?"

"No, sir, but…"

The colonel's rigid posture got even tauter—never a good sign. "But what?"

"Sir, with all due respect, I don't understand why I need a husband. I'm very capable of defending myself. I've just completed my black belt in the Marine Corps Martial Arts program."

"I'm very aware of your skills in the martial arts," the colonel said, clearly unswayed by her argument.

"Yes, sir." Her response conveyed her frustration.

Darney rolled his chair back to take a closer look at Maddy's body. As if he hadn't already checked out every luscious inch. The slimy bastard. "Marines are trained in the martial arts?"

"We study Okinawan karate, judo, tae kwon do, kung fu, boxing, and jujutsu. It gives us an edge in hand-to-hand combat, enabling Marines of every size to fight and defend themselves, despite the size of the enemy." Maddy spoke to Darney but looked directly at Hunter. What had he done to warrant those baby blues filled with animosity? He thought she was the perfect size.

"Forret, can you and Darney give me a few minutes with my men?" The colonel hadn't missed their exchange.

Forret nodded. "Sir, if there is a problem, I'm happy to team up with Jeffers."

It took all of Hunter's control not to take the jerk down. He knew exactly what Forret meant by teaming up with Maddy, and it wasn't restricted to working in the field. Hunter squeezed his hands on his thighs, trying to not react. He stood up and closed the door after the agents left.

Hunter recognized the way the colonel's square jaw clenched in silence—not a good omen for Maddy. She had been worried about being reprimanded. Now she was in the fryer, and he couldn't protect her from his superior's wrath. Marines worked as a team. Her questioning of her assignment bordered on insubordinate.

"Hines, you didn't report that there was friction between you and Jeffers."

"Sir, this is as big of a surprise to me as it is to you. I didn't know Jeffers found it difficult to work with me." He tried to keep the bitterness out of his voice but knew the colonel heard it.

"Sir, I had no trouble on my last assignment with Major

Hines. We worked well together, but I was on my own in the field. I don't see a need for us to be living in the same house."

The colonel shook his head. "These are conservative, religious women. To be accepted, you'll need to be married. It will give you more leeway, help your cover."

Hunter snorted.

"Another one of your side editorial comments, Major Hines?" Maddy chimed in a too-sweet voice.

"You think religious women are going to accept you when you dress in that kind of getup?" Hunter stared at her, trying to intimidate with his patented piercing look.

Not in the least bit daunted, Maddy bolted out of her seat and glared back. "There's nothing wrong with my clothes. If you weren't a dried-up old stick, you'd realize this is the way women dress."

Colonel Dawson chuckled. "You two are already acting like an old married couple."

Maddy's face turned beet red. She sat back down.

"Sir. For devout Muslims, the husband's word is law. As you can see, Maddy will never be able to play the part of a subservient wife." Hunter was as reluctant as Maddy to accept the assignment, albeit for very different reasons.

The colonel rubbed his square jaw with his thick fingers. "You'll only have to pretend you're married when you're seen together in public. Is that too hard for you, Jeffers?"

That he allowed her such leeway was another surprising facet of the colonel's relationship with Maddy.

"No, sir. I'll have no problem. But, sir, I'm having trouble believing Major Hines can carry off his role as a caring husband."

The colonel stood. "Your concerns have been duly noted, but this isn't a choice for either of you."

Hunter stewed over Maddy's comment. If Maddy were his, he'd take tender care of her marshmallow center *and* her hard-ass persona.

Hunter turned toward the colonel. "Is there any information suggesting that the mother and sister are involved in any way?"

The colonel shook his head. "I doubt either one has any knowledge of Hamman's activities. This is a fishing expedition to see if we can catch the big one." The colonel rose and walked toward the door, then turned back. "Seems like you both have a lot of work to do. I expect you to expunge your existence in Seattle and move into the house on Tuesday…a young couple in love. This is the new face of fighting the war on terror."

CHAPTER THREE

Maddy held her M4 carbine while she mentally shifted through what she'd need, undecided whether to bring her rifle or not. Sorting through the entire contents of her rucksack wasn't simple. Everything she owned was spread on the bedroom floor in Angie Hines's apartment while she tried to decide what might be necessary for this unusual assignment. She had no reason to take the rifle, but as a Marine, her rifle and knife were as essential as makeup and hair products for other women.

The right side of the small bedroom held the leave-behind pile, mostly items necessary for an invasion assignment such as boots, cold weather gear, GPS, chem lights, med kit, first strike rations. Finally, after way too much dithering, she placed her rifle in that pile.

On the left side were the definite-takes—her Glock, three magazines, her knife, her urban survival kit, including her Bogota Mini go-to picks, a universal handcuff key that couldn't be metal-detected, and straight and key-style shims.

Her sleep system gear wouldn't be necessary since she would be living in a house with a husband. She shook her head. This next assignment was like nothing she had ever tackled. Translating and engaging with the women would be easy; the prospect of living with Hunter left her restless and nervous. She lifted her high heels. The light, strappy shoes had been worth the forty bucks to rile up Hunter. Her inner brat was still doing a victory jig.

Angie walked into the bedroom and caught her red-handed, gloating over the high heels and the effect they had on Hunter. "Are you working undercover as a prostitute?" Angie joked, knowing Maddy couldn't share anything about her new assignment.

"No, I wore them to a meeting where I had to look the part of an office worker."

Angie snorted. "There is more to this story. You were messing with someone. And why do I get the feeling it was my brother?"

Angie did the same covert work as Maddy and, like her half-brother, was a talented intelligence agent. Maddy got a crick in her neck every time she talked to her lanky roommate. And like her brother, Angie was almost always a head taller than anyone else in the room. She also had the same jet black eyes and full lips as Hunter. The differences between the siblings were that Angie was quick to laugh and had generous curves, whereas Hunter brooded and was rock-solid muscle.

Today, the prominent dark circles around Angie's eyes looked like bruises against her yellow-olive skin. Maddy had heard Angie walking around the apartment in the middle of the night. Nightmares of IED explosions kept them both awake regularly.

Angie dropped to her butt and sat with her legs crossed on the floor next to Maddy's sleep gear, holding a floppy-eared bunny against her chest.

"Was it like when we dressed in those tight skirts and tanks to put it to Joe Hunnex?" Angie howled with a deep laugh. "The asshole kept calling us 'lesbos' under his breath."

"I'll never forget the drool on the side of his open mouth and the difficulty he had swallowing when we sashayed into the canteen. I still have those dangly earrings somewhere." Maddy grinned. "I was glad they kicked him out. He was no Marine. But I'd love to take down his two-hundred-pound flabby butt now that I have my black belt."

She and Angie had worked their asses off to prove themselves to their male counterparts. But there were times when a woman needed to use her God-given gifts and audacity to rattle the male brain bias.

"Need to level the playing field with Hunter? Shake up his detached, analytical approach?" Angie's dark eyes gleamed, showing way too much interest in Maddy's relationship with him.

Maddy didn't want to criticize Angie's brother, but since she would soon be Hunter's proxy wife and she hadn't worked out how she felt about the hunky man… "Kind of."

Angie snorted. "Fess up!"

"He's good at his job, and he's always professional, but…"

"You can tell me. He's the brother I hardly know. But it was awfully sweet that he came to help search for me."

Now it was time for Maddy to snort. "Sweet? Hunter, sweet?"

"I find it endearing to know he felt the need to protect me."

"But that's the problem. I almost prefer the sexist comments. At least you know where you stand with them. Hunter never says anything, but his dark, scrutinizing looks accuse me of not measuring up to his expectations. Somehow he doesn't see me as competent."

"Yeah, he's got that you're-a-problem look down perfectly. He uses his intense stares and size to intimidate people the same way our father did. The old man never raised his voice, but he'd give you one look and you felt two inches high. I guess it's why Hunter and I are both Marines, still trying to prove ourselves to our departed dad."

"What happened to Hunter's mom?"

"His mother split for someone in my father's battalion when Hunter was ten. Left him to be raised by our bitter father, a no-nonsense Marine."

Maddy nodded. "That explains a lot. I try not to take his coldness personally. He never openly criticizes, but he looks at me as if I'm some sort of alien, newly arrived on earth, or I'm suspected of a horrendous crime. And I'm not sure if it's because I'm a woman."

"It's definitely the woman deal. Nothing to do with your competency as a Marine. My brother has the hots for you."

"I don't believe it." Then Maddy remembered the way his wide chest hitched and his face got two bright red spots when he first saw her all gussied up in her "office" dress and shoes.

"I'm sure he has some whacked up notion about women. My dad was pretty bitter, and he fed Hunter a lot of bullshit."

"But your father married your mom. He must have loved her."

Angie shrugged. "What kid understands why their parents got married?"

Maddy flashed on her girlhood memories of her parents. She remembered they loved each other.

"My father was handsome, just like Hunter," Angie continued. "Big, muscular, black hair, with those same piercing eyes. My mom was older and lonely. I asked her once if she regretted marrying him, and all she said was if she hadn't, she wouldn't have had me. Kind of telling, huh?"

"I remember my parents laughing." Maddy remembered a lot, but now, fifteen years after their car accident, she didn't really know how much was real and how much was fantasy. But those daydreams had helped her survive in the crazy foster homes. "But I'll never know if they were truly happy."

Angie stretched her long legs "We'll miss you at meetings. Everyone keeps asking about you."

"I called Dr. Dagger and told her I'm on assignment and would be back to PTSD group as soon as I could. How are Shana and Lois?"

"Trying to forget."

Angie had suffered the most traumatic experience of those in their PTSD recovery group. She and Angie had been part of a special group of Marine women trained to gather information from the local women in Afghanistan. They were working in a small village believed to be a hiding place for the Taliban.

Angie had become friends with a sweet, young mother with soft, doe-like eyes. She hadn't spoken about what happened even once during the entire tour, but had shared the horrendous experience in their group. Angie had been waving goodbye to the mother who held her toddler in her arms when the IED exploded. Watching a child being blown to bits in front of you did things to your head. According to Dagger, seeing a child die was the most stressful of all war causalities.

"I'm tired of being 'in treatment.' I want an assignment," Angie said.

"Yeah, I wish we could work together again instead of..." She caught herself before saying "with your brother."

Maddy lifted her new suitcases. "I need to get going."

Angie forced a laugh. "I promise this time I won't go looking for you."

"I'm sorry I disappeared. The terrorist group was moving, and I had to join them without any warning. I'm sorry I caused you and everyone else the worry."

"No sweat. We all understood. And lucky you did..."

Maddy didn't want to think about how close they'd come to a bomb exploding on Pier 69. "I've got to catch a bus. Not sure when I'll be back." With suitcases in hand, Maddy left the most permanent residence she'd had in years. She was on the move again.

CHAPTER FOUR

Hunter crossed his arms and leaned against the blue rental Prius. He checked his watch, acting impatient, a man waiting for his wife to arrive. Wife? He was a professional soldier, a top-notch intelligence officer, and the idea of a wife—not any wife, but Maddy—terrified him. This assignment made Belarus and Yemen seem like child's play.

Before a dangerous mission, hours were spent in physical and psychological preparation. All possible complications were evaluated and their potential solutions considered. Like waiting during a pause in the Second Battle of Fallujah, this time he had no idea what to expect and no way to know how he'd respond to living with the spunky, sexy woman. The uncertainty left him feeling untethered and adrift, and he didn't like the sensation. The unknown, unchartered waters of this assignment sent logic and control spinning.

He had no strategies for the complication of Maddy and his inexplicable, intense, driving attraction to her. She could bring him to his knees if he allowed her. But he had to keep the upper hand. He was the ranking officer.

He leaned away from the car and spotted the #14 bus barreling down Broadway. Maddy was crisscrossing the city by bus, obscuring any link to the apartment she shared with Angie.

He had fantasized about this moment, wondering what sexy getup she'd wear to bludgeon him with her sensuality. He knew he had been the target of her sexy outfit at their last meeting, knew she was messing with his head. He got how Miss Maddy Jeffers rolled, but she had no idea who she was messing with.

The #14, jammed with commuters returning from work, pulled up to its stop at Denny and Broadway. He told himself it was the heat making his palms sweat and his heart race. He took one slow, deep breath and focused. He was a career Marine, not an adolescent having his first wet dream.

But like an adolescent, he had wondered what she slept in. T-shirts and panties? A teddy? Or did she sleep in the nude? Those thoughts and fantasies were why he'd ended up with the busty blonde barista from Starbucks last night.

The bus hissed to a stop, and the doors opened so the hot and harried passengers could file down the steps. Maddy was one of the last to exit, carrying a flowered duffel bag over her shoulder. She was definitely not Marine-issue this afternoon in her skimpy denim shorts and a white tank top that showed off her toned curves. Desire and longing for Maddy thrummed through him.

The way Maddy blew the curls off her forehead while she descended the steps told him she was hot after her long bus ride. Her head was turned to the person behind her—a big, blond guy in a tight T-shirt with bulging biceps who carried her massive suitcase. His longish blond hair hung over his eyes as he tracked Maddy's sexy walk like a hound dog. Hunter's possessiveness and anger combusted.

Maddy watched while the guy placed her matching suitcase on the sidewalk. The dude angled over her, making a slow sweep of her body. Hunter started toward them with a burning need to break up the intimate moment.

Maddy shook her head and turned toward Hunter. She waved with her fingers in a girlish, non-Maddy way, and his heart picked up speed, as did his pace. He bolted across the fifteen yards to her. He shot his best I-can-kill-you-in-less-than-ten-seconds look at the surfer dude, but the guy was either stoned or too hot on Maddy's tail to notice the danger.

Hunter stepped in front of Maddy, forcing the dude to step back. "Honey, you're late."

Maddy's eyes widened in shock.

And, without any thought, simply responding to primitive, male instincts, he pulled Maddy into his arms. He felt her stiffen when he held her tight against him and kissed her—not a slight peck but a hot, possessive "you're mine" kiss.

He was acting like a jackass, but for this mission, she was his wife and he was in charge. And he wanted that made clear. He felt her relax against him, her hands wrapping around his waist. She opened her mouth to him and pressed closer against his chest. He hadn't expected her to respond, and now all he wanted was another sweet taste of Maddy. He ran his hand along the soft dip of her hips, to her toned thigh.

The stoner dude's cough brought him to his senses. "I'm going to be heading out."

Hunter looked down at Maddy's full, pink, moist lips and waited for the moment she'd come to herself and explode. He kept his arm around her shoulder in case she had the urge to demonstrate her formidable fighting skills.

She batted those baby blues once, then twice, and then the transformation. The soft, open woman now hardened into a battle-ready Marine. She clenched and unclenched her fists at her side, and her blue eyes narrowed into a tight squint.

She pulled away and stepped closer to the dipshit who stood around like some weird voyeur. Definitely stoned. "Rod, I'm sorry for the unseemly display."

Unseemly? This from the woman who pranced her way through the JRS building looking like every man's fantasy.

"My husband hasn't seen me for a few weeks, so he's acting like a Neanderthal." She patted Hunter on the chest, getting close enough to do something painful. She gripped his hand and bent his little finger back, not enough to break it, but enough to be clear about what she thought of his manhandling her. Judging from their first day, marriage to Maddy was definitely going to be the most challenging assignment of his career.

CHAPTER FIVE

Hunter drove in silence while Maddy stewed. She had melted in Hunter Hines's arms. If the handsome brute weren't inches away, she'd pinch herself to make sure she wasn't in Kansas or some other make-believe world.

Hunter didn't merely kiss a woman, he took possession. He demanded and devoured. She could never have imagined that Hunter Hines was capable of such deep passion. Something well-hidden had emerged when Hunter kissed and held her. And she had succumbed to the desire to belong to someone. She had been alone so long.

She glanced at the man who stared straight ahead, not giving any indication of what had occurred between them. Hunter drove as masterfully as he kissed—no wasted motion, no miscalculations, despite the bumper-to-bumper traffic heading south to the Rainier Valley. Whatever he did, Hunter remained in full command.

Heat flashed through her body as she fantasized Hunter making love in his careful, demanding way.

He kept his focus on the road as he spoke. "I owe you an apology. My behavior was," he turned his head, and a small smile lifted one corner of his full, firm mouth, "unseemly."

Hunter Hines, teasing. She really might have to click her heels to yank herself back to reality.

He shrugged his massive shoulders. "I can't explain it."

Since Maddy couldn't understand her own behavior, she chose the smarter route: Silence.

He twisted to look at her again as they waited at a red light. "I've never behaved irrationally around any woman except you."

Maddy wasn't sure she liked the direction his apology was taking, implying that she was the reason he'd grabbed and kissed the bejesus out of her.

"But if we're to pretend to be married, you can't flirt with other men."

Now that was the Hunter she knew. Not the fantasy man who had kissed her.

"Flirting? Are you implying that your manhandling of me was my fault?"

"No, absolutely not." He gripped the steering wheel tightly, making the veins in his hands bulge. "It was the bozo tracking you like a hound dog on a scent."

Classic male response. The kiss hadn't been about feelings, but rather a pissing match between two alpha males. Her eyes burned with unshed tears. She rationalized that she was tired. It was the only reason his explanation hurt. Like her adolescence, she had been traveling back and forth on a city bus initially without a final destination, wondering what her next stop would be. Rather like her entire life—always moving, never settling.

Hunter made a right turn on Marion Street and parked in the shade of some alder trees across from the Renaissance-style St. James Catholic Cathedral. He shifted his long torso in the seat so his body faced hers, and he inspected her with the same careful and critical intensity that always left her confused.

"You're upset?" His voice softened.

She'd never admit to hurt feelings over such a little something.

"Look. I acted like a jerk. You in that outfit…"

Hunter always had a way of pushing the switch to incite her

to outrage and a need to do violence to his person. "My outfit? First, I'm guilty of flirting, and now it's my outfit?"

"You know you've been messing with me. Admit it. You and your hot body in that tiny, tight dress."

Maddy's mood lightened. No slouch, Hunter Hines. "FYI. You need to look around. That dress is what every other woman is wearing." She turned in her seat to look closer at his face. She got a whiff of hot male and his woodsy pine aftershave. With Hunter's big frame squeezed into the small front seat, if she turned and lifted her legs, she'd be straddling his lap. She wanted to reach out and run her finger along the dark stubble on his jaw.

He leaned against the door, retreating from their closeness. His face was flushed, and he kept swallowing, his strong throat rippling. "Maddy, you've lived with Marines. All I'm saying is men respond to women in revealing clothes. It's part of our DNA."

After basic training, she knew more about the inner workings of the male brain and its sex drive then she'd ever wanted to. "Got it. Because you're a male, you can't control your urges. And with the city filled with women in shorts and tank tops for the summer, you can't stop yourself from grabbing them and kissing them silly."

His dark eyes narrowed and that full upper lip flattened. Why did she enjoy baiting this sexy grizzly bear?

She leaned closer and touched his muscular thigh. "It's okay, Hunter. Do you think I want to make this marriage real?"

"What?" He sat up straight and hit his head on the ceiling. Then he laughed, a deep belly laugh that started in his chest and rolled down his tight abs. He put both hands up in the air. "You got me, Maddy."

"I do?" Maddy batted her eyelashes like the heroine in a melodrama.

He shook his head and grinned. She had never seen Hunter smile in such a spontaneous, open way before. The grin spread across his face and lightened his shadowy eyes. His enjoyment did wonderful and twisty things to her stomach, like a sudden steep drop on a roller coaster.

"Truce, Maddy? I'll try to control my primitive urges when I'm around you." He looked down at her breasts, examining every exposed inch of her bare skin while his fingers twitched on his thighs.

Her lungs tightened as if there wasn't enough air in the car. The blood pulsed in gushes through her body.

"As long as you don't flaunt yourself."

Flaunt? She readied herself to blast the idiot, karate-style—fully focused, kill energy. "Hunter…" And suddenly she couldn't stop the laugh that bubbled upward. "How can I bitch at you if I don't know your full name?"

"Huh?" The bewildered look on his usually intense face made her laugh harder. "If we're married, I should know your middle name."

His dark eyes lit up like his sister's. "James. Hunter James Hines."

"Oh, that's nice. Hunter James Hines." She laughed again at the confused look on his face. "Now I can't remember what I was going to yammer at you about."

He chuckled. An easy, relaxed sound that vibrated in the car and in her heart. Their eyes met, and she leaned toward him as he moved closer. She stilled with anticipation. The only sound was their erratic breathing. His loud and rough, hers quick and impatient. He stared into her eyes as he tucked one of her wayward curls behind her ear. She felt suspended by his fierce look and the gentle touch.

"What's your middle name, my ball and chain?"

She huffed. "Ball and chain?"

With his long finger, he traced the outside of her ear, and sensations skittered along her skin like sand blowing along the beach. She leaned closer, wanting to feel his hard body against hers again.

He pulled his hand back as if touching her brought pain. "We can't do this." His breath and words were choppy. "I've got to keep my hands off of you. It's this weird assignment, pretending we're married. It's messed up."

She had told herself all the same things repeatedly, so why did it hurt when he said it? It was exactly like her adolescence with each foster home—a temporary family. This isn't forever. Not a family to love or be loved by.

She moved back into her seat and watched the people walking through the cathedral's thick, twelve-foot doors. "Don't worry about it. We can have a no-touch, no-feelings rule in this pretend marriage of ours."

He turned quickly to look at her, to give her one of his dark stares. "Speaking of pretend marriages, I picked up a wedding ring for you. I wasn't sure about your size, but I knew it had to be tiny." He pulled a square, black jewelry box from the front pocket of his blue oxford shirt. No T-shirts and shorts for Hunter.

It was then she noticed he wore a gold wedding band on his left hand. Seeing the wedding band that marked him as belonging to her awakened the little shards of loneliness and isolation buried deep in her soul.

This wasn't real. This wasn't about caring. The gesture only meant the man paid attention to detail.

Hunter opened the box and took out an exquisite opal in a simple silver setting. "I hope you'll like it."

Her throat thickened, and she couldn't speak. She had no words for the excess of new emotions and old pain twisting inside of her. "I've never had anything this beautiful." The ring reminded her of her mother's engagement ring—the one her foster sibling had stolen.

"The way the colors change reminded me of the blue in your eyes, the fluctuation with your moods from bright sunny blue to stormy purple."

Maddy swallowed against all the emotion stuck in her throat.

No one ever paid attention to her or her eyes. No one had cared that her most meaningful possession had been taken from her.

He took her hand into his giant palm and slid the ring onto her finger. He was looking down, but his cheeks had reddened. "For my pretend wife."

She was asking for a lot of hurt if she mistook this ring for her own romantic fantasies. Like her mother's ring, this one would disappear, too. She didn't—couldn't—believe in happily ever after. She had learned the harsh reality at the age of fourteen, and no child could continue believing in fantasies after her parents died.

She'd never let herself be that vulnerable again.

Grief washed through her over the inevitable loss of the ring on her finger and the man who'd tenderly placed it there. "Will you be able to return the ring when we're finished with the assignment?"

Hunter stiffened and started the car. "Don't worry about it." And he drove away from the shade of the alders and the moment of make-believe.

CHAPTER SIX

Hunter pulled up in front of a small farmhouse in the densely populated Rainier Valley, the area where the beautiful people of Seattle didn't live. Recent immigrants and the working poor resided in South Seattle. "We're home."

Maddy leaned forward to catch a better glimpse of the house. "Oh, my God. It's nothing like I expected. It looks like Snow White's cottage tucked in the woods. How can such a charming, rustic home sit in the middle of all these fabricated '70s houses?"

"This whole area used to be cherry orchards and farmland."

"Really?" Her blue eyes widened. "But there is a 7-Eleven, a psychic, and a hair salon on the next block. We're in the middle of the 'hood."

"Now, yes, but years ago, the valley was called Garlic Gulch or Wop City because of the Italian immigrants. I've heard both from our neighbor."

"You met our neighbor?"

"Pretty hard not to. She came out when I brought in the groceries. She is the only English-speaking person on the block. She has lived here for fifty years and has seen the neighborhood go through many changes. None for the better, if you ask her."

"I don't care. I love the house, the flowers in the window boxes, and the chairs on the front porch. I've always wanted…"

Hunter watched her transformation. She shifted from enthusiastic to remote, slamming shut her feelings. For a brief moment, she was the open girl she probably had been before her childhood world had become untrustworthy. Trust didn't come any easier for him, since he'd learned that mothers weren't forever. It was why they both excelled at their jobs. They were suspicious of everyone.

Maddy gazed out the window, like a child watching the first snowfall of the season. "Why would anyone leave this house?"

"The young couple who lives here was transferred to New York for the next three months. Or that's the story I was told. If you're asked, we're renting until we find our own house."

"We'll be here for three months?"

He couldn't decipher if the news pleased her. She twisted a curl around her finger, and her shoulders hunched.

Three months of sharing the same house with Maddy, sleeping in the next room. He wasn't sure if he could survive it. He let her believe it was all about sex when he'd kissed her, knowing she believed the BS that all guys are randy.

He'd made it all about her hot little body, but there was much more to his attraction to her. Maddy was the quirkiest mix of strength and softness and vulnerability that he had ever seen in a woman. He admired her loyalty to her friends, her job, and her country. It didn't take a shrink to understand his need for a loyal woman. Maddy had it in spades.

"Now the act begins." Except, for him, this didn't feel like an act.

Maddy put her hand on the door handle. He reached over and covered her hand with his. "Don't get out. Let me open it for you. I'm a man in love."

He came around the Prius and opened her door, offering his hand to help her out. She rolled her big, wide eyes at him and extended her hand. "There is no one on the street to see us."

"The nosy neighbor across the street is watching from her front window. She is going to be a problem."

He leaned down into the car to be face-to-face. "Maddy."

"Yes?" She looked up at him with a question in her big baby blues.

"Get ready for a bit of PDA."

"PDA?"

He pulled her against him and kissed her lightly on her lips.

Caught off guard for a second, she stiffened as he pressed her against him, holding her tight in his arms. Unaffected by his embrace, she talked around his gentle kiss. "If you touch my ass, I'll nut you."

He laughed out loud, shocking himself. He never wanted this marriage or this assignment to end.

A smiling and relaxed Maddy sat across from him at the polished pine dining room table. The furnishings were like the house, filled with rustic, old-fashioned charm. Maddy ate her dinner of steak and a baked potato with gusto. For such a petite woman, Maddy packed in a lot of calories. Probably to make up for her time living on the streets during her last assignment.

He wasn't sure if it was the meat and potatoes, the Oregon Pinot Noir, or his company that made her look replete. He hoped it was a little bit of everything. Maddy deserved to be treated well, and while she was his wife, he planned to pamper her. Not that he'd ever tell her, or she might threaten to nut him again.

"I can't remember the last time I sat down to eat a home-cooked meal."

"The ecoterrorists didn't dine out much?"

Maddy giggled, a light, youthful sound that made him smile. "Unlike the Seahawks, we didn't dine out on twenty-four-ounce steaks."

She did that a lot to him. Lightened his mood with her irreverent and simple enjoyment. Since meeting Maddy, Hunter had smiled more than he had his whole lifetime.

"Thank you for cooking. Doing all this, shopping, planning. It is so nice here. Not the usual assignment."

He didn't want to think about what Maddy had suffered during her past assignments or as a foster child. He wanted to take care of her, make her world a safe and better place. For the first time, he wanted little Maddy Jeffers to experience what it was like to be loved and protected.

Hunter leaned back in the small hardwood chair. Sometimes old-world charm could be downright uncomfortable. "I didn't do much, just grilled, but I do like to cook."

Maddy's cheeks were now a rosy pink, but he wasn't sure if it was from the wine or the heat of the summer night. He had opened all the windows and the door, but it was an unusually hot summer in the Northwest.

She leaned forward with her elbows on the table. "You like to cook? Is there anything you can't do?"

Smile spontaneously, feel a deep connection with a woman, fall in love. "There are loads of things I can't do."

"Name one, besides relax, hang out, or tell a joke." She gave him the saucy look he enjoyed.

"Little do you know." Talking with Maddy brought out a youthful side to him. He wanted to tease back, make her laugh, have her appreciate him as more than a tight-ass soldier. "Angie didn't tell you I had a gig as a stand-up comedian before I joined the Marines."

Maddy laughed out loud, making the curls bounce across her forehead. Tears were in her eyes, and she covered her mouth with one hand. "It's mind-boggling. The image is too funny."

"But that's why my act worked. Pretending I was an uptight guy versus my raunchy, weird self actually worked. I was invited to go to Las Vegas."

Maddy tapped her finger against her cheek. "I can't tell if you're messing with me or not."

"Only a little bit. I like to see you laugh. And finding humor in our work is the only way to last in this job. You have to see entertainment in the craziest crap."

Maddy's lips curved into a small smile. "You do that?"

"What?"

"Find absurdity in your assignments."

"I try to, but you know, on the whole, Marines aren't exactly the joking kind. But I've found I can make jokes with a few of the men. And you have to admit this pretend marriage is pretty amusing."

The brightness in Maddy's eyes darkened. "What's so funny?"

"I'm a single man living with a hot woman on an assignment that requires me to touch and kiss her."

"Hard work for you, huh?" The mischievous Maddy was back.

"Joking aside, I don't want to make you uncomfortable. I'm a normal man, and you're one sexy woman." He tried to keep his voice neutral, but he could hear the desperation showing through. "You need to relax and enjoy this home. You're coming off a tough assignment. I promise not to hit on you." *Only in every one of my fantasies.* "But you have to promise one thing. You wear pajamas, because I don't think I can handle any sexy teddies or camisoles or any other lingerie." It took all his self-control not to ask if she slept in the buff.

Maddy had gone silent. Her eyes searched his face. Maddy was trained in espionage and in the military. She knew how men's minds worked.

"No problem. I bought PJs at Target before I started this assignment. But you have to promise me you won't be walking around in your Trophy Boy thongs."

"Thongs? For boys?" His voice was high-pitched. And the way Maddy giggled and her eyes danced told him she was delighted by his shock.

She kept snickering. The Pinot was definitely getting to her. "You don't wear boy thongs? I had you pegged as a thong guy."

There was her devilish mix of tease and candor. She was the most outrageously perfect woman.

He threaded his fingers through his hair to keep from grabbing her and kissing her until she wanted him as much as he wanted her. *Bad plan.* He wasn't going to behave like an out-of-control lecher—not give in to his desire. No way. He could be tough as steel when he needed to be. He was a Marine. He was always in control.

What a load of crap. He hadn't been in control since he met Maddy Jeffers.

CHAPTER SEVEN

Maddy was more nervous today than her first day at Mercer Middle School. After being introduced by the director of the program, Maddy stood before the circle of Afghan women at the Women's Refuge Project. As the enthusiastic, matronly woman explained that their regular teacher's absence was due to a family illness and Maddy would be filling in, the Muslim women spoke in hushed voices and stared at their new teacher.

In the Middle East and Asia, staring at strangers wasn't considered rude, and these women had the stare down to an art form. Their dark eyes assessed every part of Maddy, from her blond curls to her white, long-sleeve blouse, black, calf-length skirt, and her ballet flats.

Maddy refused to squirm, but middle school memories of cruel looks from the cool girls whose clothes hadn't been from Goodwill flashed through her with every intrusive perusal.

Before she'd left this morning, Hunter had teased her about finally dressing the way he wanted his wife to dress. She had shot back, calling him a male chauvinistic pig. And they laughed together. She was amazed at how easily the banter was developing between them. Last night and this morning had been way too cozy and comfortable. After a sleepless night, she was focused on the work and not her tempting husband.

Maddy greeted the ten women in Dari. Ruth, the teacher she'd replaced, had shared that all the women spoke Dari and many also spoke Pashto. Afghanistan had two major languages, and lucky for Maddy, she was most proficient in Dari. Ruth had also advised her that the women practiced a range of religious observances that often led to tension in the discussions.

The FBI had provided her with the passport pictures of Abu Abdul Hamman's mother and sister. The images were of limited value, though, since the Hamman women were always covered by their burkas. It'd be next to impossible for a modern American woman to read their facial reactions or easily strike up a friendship with them. She'd decided to focus on developing a connection with the younger woman first.

Maddy scanned the group. It was easy to discern the differences in the women's religious and world views from the range of headgear. Four of the women wore niqabs, veils that covered the face, revealing only the area around the eyes. Three young women in American attire of blue jeans and blouses wore the hijab, a square scarf that covered the head and neck but left the face unobstructed.

Abu's mother, Guli, and his sister, Sadia, were the only ones in burkas, the most concealing of all Islamic veils, which covered their entire faces and bodies, leaving only a mesh screen to see through.

Maddy had decided to alter the curriculum schedule. Today she planned to discuss food shopping and restaurants, hoping to bring up Abu's restaurant and the women's role in assisting him. The purpose of the classes was to help the women negotiate everyday barriers inherent in a foreign culture and language. Of course, the additional prohibition against speaking with any male outside the family made adapting to American society more difficult.

She started with an icebreaker to warm up the group, inviting each woman to introduce herself and identify one thing that was hard about her adjustment to American living.

She began on her far right so Guli and Sadia would speak last, giving her a chance to observe their body language and see how they reacted to the other women. Guli, the mother, sat stiffly, hidden and removed from the group, as did her daughter, Sadia.

Many of the women cited how fast everyone spoke English. Two of the women described their children's frustration that their mothers were so slow in learning the new language. The other women laughed, but neither Guli nor Sadia engaged with the group. Sadia whispered her introduction and said that everything in America was as she'd expected.

Guli's strident, sharp tone stopped the women's chatting. She spoke disdainfully about Americans wanting them to adjust so they would forget their ways, forget their country, the observance of their religion. She pointedly stared at the young women in blue jeans. The silence in the room was tense and awkward. Knowing that Guli's husband had been killed by a drone, Maddy sympathized with her feelings, to a point. It was paradoxical that the mother and daughter attended the classes to help them acculturate, when obviously the mother didn't approve of American ways.

At the end of the class, Maddy stood at the door to thank each woman for attending the class and tell them she looked forward to seeing them tomorrow. Guli didn't acknowledge her, but Sadia nodded her head as she passed.

This morning, she had been so hopeful about her ability to relate to the women. She had made a connection with all of them but Abu's family. She learned nothing about Abu's restaurant, but today's class wasn't a total waste. She had learned that Abu's mother and sister, like all the women, shopped at the Columbia City Farmer's Market on Wednesday. Because of their adherence to their conservative practices, Guli and Sadia most likely would be at the market with a male.

Field work took patience and time. She was short on both. She didn't know how long she could last on this mission when it required resisting a charming Hunter Hines. It had been easier to resist him when she considered him a rigid, humorless man.

At least for today, she and Hunter would go to the market to observe Abu and his family, and then she'd insist they eat dinner at a restaurant. Last night's dinner had been too intimate and too wonderful. It made a girl want things she couldn't have.

CHAPTER EIGHT

Hunter took Maddy's hand as they got closer to the Columbia City Farmer's Market. He loved taking advantage of any excuse to touch her. They walked hand in hand down the last two blocks on Rainier Avenue before the market.

The low-income community to the north was being transformed by art collectives, used bookstores, upscale restaurants, and, of course, a yoga and cross-fit center—all the requirements for gentrification. All that was missing was an upscale gelato and whiskey bar, and this neighborhood would look like the rest of homogenized Seattle.

Maddy pulled on his hand. "Is all this PDA necessary? No one buys you as the doting husband type."

"Why do you say that? What does a doting husband look like?"

"Not someone who scowls all the time."

"What you call a scowl, I prefer to label a focused look." He squeezed her hand. "Really, I can't remember the last time I gave my focused look." Because of Maddy, he now spent a lot of time smiling. "Maybe this morning, when my wife didn't make me coffee."

Maddy chuckled. "This wife is not making coffee."

"You won't cook for your husband?"

"I don't have a husband. And if I did have a husband, he'd make coffee for me and serve it in bed." A crimson flush crept across Maddy's cheeks, matching the heat rushing through him. "I...never mind."

He stopped on the sidewalk and wanted to kiss her, but instead played the part he had been assigned. "The husband you choose will be happy to serve you breakfast in bed every morning after—"

She pulled at his hand. "Don't you dare say anything else." Her chest rose and fell in hurried breaths.

He was glad to know he wasn't the only one affected by their sleeping arrangement. He hardly slept last night, tossing and turning and on alert for any sound from Maddy. "As you pointed out, I excel at many things once I determine my goal. I'd put my whole heart and every other part of me into making my wife happy. She'd be the recipient of all my devotion, skill, and undivided attention."

Maddy tugged again on his hand, trying to back away from the intensity between them. He wanted her to know how he'd provide for her. It was important that she understand how devoted he'd be.

Maddy cleared her throat. "I'm sure you'll make someone a very good husband. But right now, you're my pretend husband, and three of the young women from my class are coming this way."

He looked up and tried to switch gears from the playful teasing. Maddy kept him distracted. Not good for a risky assignment. Two young women, dressed like any other mid-twenties American women, except for scarves hiding their hair, were with a traditionally-dressed Muslim woman, the three walking toward them at the entrance to the market. The woman with her face partially covered by niqab carried a curly-haired, chubby toddler in her arms.

Maddy greeted them by name in Dari as she introduced him to the women. The women averted their eyes and didn't acknowledge him. Hunter nodded and stepped back away from the women in polite acknowledgment of their cultural requirement that he not get too close.

Interesting that Maddy hadn't hesitated to introduce her

husband to the women, behaving as any married woman would. The colonel had been right; it did strengthen Maddy's cover to have a husband.

The proud mother offered the toddler to Maddy, and a smile wreathed Maddy's face with joy as she took the chunky boy into her arms. The baby carefully inspected Maddy's eyes and hair while she smiled and cooed to him in a high-pitched, singsong voice. As Maddy bent her head to tickle his chubby stomach, the rascal grabbed Maddy's hair, his little fist wrapping around one her curls. Maddy laughed as he held tight.

His mother tried to unwrap his fist, but the boy giggled, playing with Maddy's curls as if they were a new toy.

Maddy continued to laugh, her face alight, and Hunter was mesmerized by her sheer pleasure in the little boy. He moved close and took the soft, chubby fist into his hand. The youngster looked up at him in surprise, his round, black eyes studying Hunter intently. Hunter wouldn't have touched a female child, but even at this young age, boys were allowed more freedom.

Hunter spoke in Dari. "You want to go up?"

Hunter checked the mother's face before taking the boy into his arms. The mother beamed at him, grinning broadly at her son's antics. Hunter took the frisky child and lifted him up in the air. "You like to go high?"

The boy giggled as Hunter swung him down in one swoop and raised him high in the air again. "You want again?" The boy's wide smile was enough for Hunter to continue the game several more times before realizing that all the women were watching with admiration.

He smiled sheepishly at Maddy, who studied him with apparent fascination while nibbling on her lower lip.

The mother lifted her toddler back into her arms. The little guy glanced back and forth between Maddy and Hunter, clearly wanting more playtime with his human toys. The Afghan women smiled shyly and then spoke softly to Maddy, urging her to have a baby of her own. Maddy kept her head down; the women kept stealing peeks at him.

After watching Maddy with the boy, he wondered if she wanted to have children. He needed to pull himself together, because he was fantasizing about having a fat toddler with blond curls who looked and smiled just liked Maddy. He wasn't filled with his usual dread at the idea of motherly love, because he knew Maddy would never abandon a child. Never.

One of the young women looked beyond Hunter and spoke low in Pashto, unaware that Hunter and Maddy understood both Afghan languages. Suddenly, all the laughter and spontaneity vanished as the woman grew silent.

He paused before turning to see who had such a dampening effect on the women. Two women in burkas, accompanied by a smiling Abu Abdul Hamman in a long-sleeve shirt and casual pants, approached their group. Nothing else was said, but the playfulness of the past moments promptly disappeared.

Tension prickled along his spine. He could almost smell the approach of danger; their quarry was near.

The women, including Maddy, separated themselves from him to greet Abu's mother and sister.

It took all Hunter's control to comply with the prohibitions and step away from Maddy and the possible danger.

With his mother and sister several steps behind him, Abu walked directly toward Hunter as if he recognized him. Abu's mother and sister joined the women, who huddled together and spoke in hushed tones.

Abu bowed his head and then offered his hand. Hunter shook his hand and waited in politeness.

"My mother and sister have informed me of your wife's dedication to helping our women."

Was there sarcasm or a veiled threat in Abu's comment? This was playing out exactly as they had hoped. They had established contact with Abu, but the man was effusive and friendly. Hunter acted nonchalant and focused on monitoring the subtext of the polite conversation. Talking to a Westerner would be all about courteous form and nothing of substance.

"My wife is very dedicated to helping others."

Abu smiled broadly, revealing an uneven and crooked front tooth. He had a long scar over his left eye that Hunter recognized as a knife injury. The Afghans were very skilled with knives as weapons, honed over years of battle with many invaders.

"Yes? It is a good quality in a wife. I have heard that you live in our neighborhood and that you both worked in our country with the Red Cross?"

"Yes, that is how I met my wife."

"Your wife helped with reuniting families torn apart by the war. But what work did you do?" Abu inspected Hunter, his eyes narrowing slightly as he scanned his face.

Hunter's body clamped in awareness. There was nothing in Abu's placid smile that betrayed suspicion.

"I was working on a water project. I'm an engineer. You have a beautiful country."

"Yes, nothing compares to our mountains. You must come to my restaurant. We serve authentic Afghan food. My Afghan pilaf and lamb kebabs are the best in the city."

"Thank you. I'd love to bring Maddy. She misses the incredible Afghan food." He had no idea if Maddy actually ate Afghan food after her two tours of duty.

Hunter turned to the shout of a woman's voice from behind him. "Hey, Henry. I didn't think I'd see you so soon."

It didn't take but a mini-second to realize that his ass was about to be burned. Amy, the barista from Starbucks, in a tight black skirt and low-cut white blouse, strutted toward him. He bowed his head to excuse himself. Abu gave him a knowing look. Such communications went beyond language and cultural barriers. Male lust was global.

The women had all stopped speaking at Amy's brash shout. All female eyes turned and tracked Amy's sensual walk and voluptuous adaptation of the Starbuck's uniform. Women's intuition about "other women" was also global. Maddy did a double take and then gave Hunter a close-lipped smile before she straightened and turned her back.

Hunter took Amy's elbow and led her away from the women and Abu. He hadn't told Amy anything that could compromise his cover, but he couldn't take any risks.

She chuckled in a deep, husky voice. "Henry, you're not happy to see me?"

No kidding. Like having needles stuck in his eyes. Amy had been a mistake. A big fricking mistake. He never made poor judgement calls. Not until Maddy. For the first time in his life, he was in over his head dealing with one woman. A glance back told him Maddy's spine was Marine tight, and he imagined her chin was thrust forward in battle stance.

"Look, I explained it was a mistake. You and I shouldn't have happened. I apologize. You were great."

Now all the closeness and intimacy he and Maddy were starting to share had evaporated because of a brief lapse in judgement.

"But Henry, nothing happened. And you were such a gentleman, and I can't stop thinking about peeling you out of those clothes… And. You know how great it would be between us."

He shook his head. He was tired of hookups with no attachments. He was ready for more than a night of hard, grinding sex.

Hunter moved Amy farther away from Maddy and out of earshot. He needed this whole mess to end. He was on assignment, and somehow, his personal life was affecting the mission in a dangerous, unpredictable way.

"Look," he said, "it's never going to happen. And I don't want you to think it might. I was a total jackass to come on to you that night." He hadn't come on to Amy; she had been all over him when he went in to get an iced tea after moving the surveillance equipment into the house. She even offered to give him a blow job in the bathroom. But as frustrated as Maddy had him, he couldn't accept Amy's offer for quick relief.

Amy moved closer and touched his chest where his shirt opened. "I get it, but if you ever change your mind…"

As if Maddy had eyes in the back of her head, she turned right as Amy's fingers wandered down his shirt. Maddy turned her back again.

He took Amy's wandering hands from his chest. "Sorry, Amy. You deserve someone who cares about you."

"Tell me about it." She gave a self-deprecating, throaty laugh and then dropped her hand. "Next time, Henry. I've got to get back to work." She strutted past Abu and the women and kept on walking…and then she turned and did a little finger wave for Maddy and the women's benefit. "See you around."

With Amy gone, the women all turned to stare at him. Their admiration and shy looks were gone. He knew he was scowling, but he didn't care. He felt like a ridiculous adolescent caught in a bad high school scene.

Maddy hadn't moved. The women moved closer to Maddy in a protective cluster. He was the bad guy in this scenario, and there was no other way to play it. Except he and Maddy weren't married, and he hadn't done anything wrong…except be a horny guy who got offered dirty sex.

Maddy said her goodbyes to the women, smiling and gently touching the baby's head as one last gesture. His stomach twisted in knots with the urgent desire to explain everything.

Why should he care that much about Maddy's reaction? Because he would never dream of hurting or embarrassing her. She deserved only the best from her pretend husband.

CHAPTER NINE

Maddy excused herself, ignoring the women's sympathetic looks. Like many women betrayed before her, she reached deep into the primitive well of pride to prevent anyone from seeing her pain. She plastered a smile across her face while hurt coiled around her heart. She tried to remind herself this was a pretend relationship and shouldn't matter. But she couldn't feel betrayed unless she actually cared for the callous brute.

She put her hand on his arm. "Honey, we should get our shopping done." She didn't make eye contact with Abu, since it was not her place to approach a man.

Hunter flinched at her touch. What was he expecting…a jealous lover scene? They were undercover, and Abu would expect a wife to ignore a husband's mistress. If she were a real wife and not undercover, her reaction would be a totally different kettle of sharks.

Hunter took her arm and linked it under his. "Mr. Hamman. May I introduce my wife?"

Abu bowed his head. "Mrs. Grady."

Maddy nodded in acknowledgment.

"Your husband has been telling me how much you love our country and miss the food. I hope you both will come to my restaurant, Afghan Kebab. It is on the corner of Graham and Rainier."

"Thank you, Mr. Hamman. Your restaurant is very close to where we live."

"Yes, that is what my sister informed me. You must come and have my *gosh-e-feel*—like American elephant ear pastries."

"If my husband has time, it would be an honor." Her face and throat hurt from the fake sweet tone and fake sweet smile.

Abu's black eyes lightened. He hadn't missed the little wifely jab, which Maddy thought he might expect from a jealous wife.

Everyone bowed.

Hunter led her toward the fruit stand. "Shall we get some cherries? They look fabulous."

"I'd like some blueberries."

Although the group had dispersed, she was very aware that her students were observing her and Hunter. They walked arm in arm down the long aisle of organic farmers. She played the part of a doting wife. She even went on tiptoe and whispered in her husband's ear as a sweet romantic gesture. "Abu and his mother and sister have left. Let's get the hell out of here."

"I thought you wanted to try La…something, the Italian place, for dinner tonight."

"No, I'm going to get cheese and a baguette for dinner. It's all I need." *No more romantic meals where you charm me with great food, wine, jokes, intense gazes, and make me believe.*

They walked along Rainier Avenue in silence until they got past the crowds. Hunter carried the bags loaded with fruit, cheese, fresh pasta, bread, and a bouquet of sunflowers. Hunter had insisted on buying her flowers. This farce was getting ridiculous. As if a betrayed wife would forget and forgive adultery with flowers. She had to remind herself this wasn't a marriage.

Maddy hated women who pouted, and she wasn't one of them. Hunter had been very clear after he'd kissed her voraciously. Men had needs, and since she wasn't available, he looked elsewhere. "Did you get any helpful information from Abu? He was pleasant enough. No dark looks of censure for a mere woman."

"I agree. Abu is very charming. And very polite. But during

my time in Afghanistan and Iraq, I learned that politeness is a public behavior and unrelated to how people actually feel about you."

"Yes, it's the same with the women."

"He asked where we live."

"In class, Rasa, the woman with the cute baby, asked where we live. I shared how we just moved to the neighborhood, making it natural for us to innocently bump into Abu and his family."

"He was very interested in our work with ICRC. Did you tell the women anything different than we discussed? I didn't want to contradict what you had said."

"I was very sketchy. Keep the lies close to the truth, right? I emphasized how I fell in love with my husband in their country. Women always want to hear love stories, how the couple met, how the man proposed."

Hunter stopped on the sidewalk, amusement and something else in his voice. "You're a romantic?"

Maddy kept walking. *I'm a Marine on assignment.* She repeated the mantra in her head to match the rhythm of her dogged walk. As Hunter had said from the beginning, this pretend marriage was messed up. Nothing to do with real feelings; an assignment, that's all. Once this was finished, she'd hope to never see Hunter again. With her resolve restored, she lifted her chin and marched down Rainier Avenue to their house, where she would stay in her room with no more intimate dinners or moments with Hunter.

"Maddy, wait up." Hunter took two big steps toward her. His hands were full with the bags, so he couldn't touch her with his bogus PDA.

He had his usual scowl back in place. She should remember her first impression of him—a tighty-whities dude—before he started all the nice, husbandly gestures. She twisted the ring on her finger, wanting to take it off and throw it at him, but something held her back.

"Maddy, we need to talk about that woman, but not here."

With her brisk pace and her combusting emotions, perspiration beaded up on her face, and her long-sleeve blouse stuck to her skin. All she wanted was a shower and to get away from Hunter. Surprisingly, the giant man showed no signs of the heat or the stress of a public meeting with his sweetie.

Relieved to be at the house and out of the sun, she hurried down the brick walkway to the front porch. How quickly perspectives could change. This morning she had found the little farmhouse enchanting, and now? A brief stopover in her history of endless wandering.

Hunter dropped the bags on one of the Adirondack chairs and unlocked the front door. He held the door so Maddy could enter first. Maddy felt his stare on her back as she walked into the living room. The overstuffed chintz couch and wicker furniture now seemed sickeningly saccharine. "I'm going to jump in the shower. I need to get into something cooler." *And I need time away from you and your bullshit ways.*

"Go ahead and shower. But you can't run away. We have to talk about what happened."

Did he see her as someone who ran away from her problems? Maybe when she was sixteen and had no other choice, but not anymore. She turned quickly and stepped back into the living room. "Okay, let's talk."

"You sure you don't want that shower? You look pretty hot."

She was hot—hot under the collar and ready to take down a certain womanizing jerk.

"I can wait. Let's hear what you think I'm avoiding."

He rubbed his massive hand back and forth over the stubble on his chin. She was starting to like the less polished Hunter. He was such a dark man that by afternoon he needed to shave again. It was funny how she was starting to notice all the little things that came with living together.

"I almost blew our cover back there. This isn't like me. I never depart from my assignment. Your safety and this mission are more important than my personal feelings. I need us to get back on track."

Maddy picked up one of the bags of groceries and walked to the kitchen to avoid Hunter's careful scrutiny. "What you do during this assignment is your business." She dug into the bag for the creamy goat' cheese. "Your girlfriend helped my relationship with the women. The colonel was right—a husband, even an unfaithful husband—really does strengthen my cover."

Hunter followed her into the kitchen and stood close behind her. Heat radiated off his massive frame. "Girlfriend?" She felt his hot breath on her neck. "Have I been acting like I have a girlfriend?"

She swirled around. "How would I know how you act when you have a girlfriend? But don't sweat it." She turned back to the groceries and spoke over her shoulder. "Your affair is helpful—for the women to see an American woman being taken for granted builds camaraderie."

He grabbed her arm and turned her toward him. His voice was raw. "You think I'd be the kind of husband who would cheat on his wife?"

His angular face was stark with emotion. She hadn't meant to bring up the old pain of his mother's abandonment. She understood wounds that scarred but never healed. "Sorry, I know you'd be faithful." Her stomach got a funny, quirky feeling at the idea of Hunter as a devoted husband and father.

His wide chest expanded deeply. He leaned closer, as if to kiss her, then reached around and grabbed the cherries out of the grocery bag. The only sound was his harsh breathing. "I'm here to protect you. I could have ruined our cover because of my need…" He dumped the bag of cherries into a colander.

Not wanting him to see how his words affected her, she bent down to throw the pasta and veggies into the frig. "I do not need to hear about your sex with that woman."

He turned away from the sink to glare at her. "You find it hard to believe that women are attracted to me?"

Oh, she believed it. She saw the way the woman had drooled over him.

He took a deep breath and shook his head. "I didn't have sex with that woman. Because of you."

She stood up suddenly and bumped her head on the freezer door which had swung open. "Ow! What?"

He turned and opened the cupboard. With his back to her, he growled. "My greedy, crazy, over-the-top need for you drove me… Forget it." He took a vase off the top shelf and turned toward her. "We need to get this job done. Everything else has to wait. My gut is telling me there is more to the Hamman family."

Maddy's heart beat harder, faster replaying Hunter's words.

"You can't leave me hanging like this. You're greedy? Crazy? That doesn't sound like the man who said women don't matter when it came to men's sex drive."

"Right." He used a large Japanese chopping knife to hack off the end of the sunflowers, his head bent forward, accentuating the taut muscles in his back and neck. His words were clipped, matching his precise whacks. "Doesn't matter."

Was the man clueless? Maddy's voice came out squeaky. "You barely know me."

Hunter dropped the knife and took three steps, backing her up against the refrigerator. He leaned close, so close she inhaled the smell of aroused male mixed with his woodsy pine aftershave.

"I've been following your career since I found out you were Angie's best friend."

The stainless steel door was cool and hard, just like the look Hunter shot at her. "But…but you hardly have any contact with Angie."

"Doesn't mean I wasn't looking out for her. She's my sister."

Maddy lowered her eyes, avoiding his probing scrutiny. One assumption about Hunter after another was crumbling. She gave a half-hearted laugh. "Marines take care of their own."

His full lower lip curved into a little smile as he toyed with one of her curls. "I think you'd take care of your own even if they weren't Marines."

His face was inches from hers, and she could see little flecks of amber in his nearly black eyes. "Why didn't you ever tell me?"

"I assumed you knew from our last assignment that I'd find out everything about you. I have access to all your files."

Maddy gulped around the panic rising in her throat. She was chosen to go undercover with the ecoterrorism group because she had lived on the streets after running away from her last foster family. She hadn't really considered that Hunter could, or would, read all her files, know about her whacked adolescence, her disastrous foster families, and her drug-dealing boyfriend.

He raised her chin with his finger. "There is nothing to be ashamed of. You pulled yourself out of a bad situation. I admired your grit even before I met you, and more ever since I met you." He traced his finger along her chin. His voice roughened. "I knew I was in trouble."

She couldn't breathe. The air had been sucked out of the kitchen.

"I've been in trouble since the day you came bouncing into my life. Nothing is the same. You're a hot woman with incredible integrity and honesty."

Maddy stared at this giant alpha male—muscles bunched, raven-black hair messy from running his fingers through it, strong jaw covered in black stubble. This was the complicated, difficult man who barely spoke and only gave her disapproving looks. Now he stared at her with burning need.

With his rough fingers, he traced her cheek and down her throat, sending shivers skittering along her damp skin. "Having you in the next bedroom was pushing me over the edge. I went into Starbucks after moving a lot of our stuff into the house, and Amy came on to me. I wanted to get my head screwed back on so I could do my job. I thought… Well, you get the gist."

Maddy searched his face. "You really didn't do anything with her?"

He smoothed her hair away from her face. "I couldn't. She wasn't you."

She felt trembly all over, behind her knees and in her stomach. But she couldn't make herself look away from his burning gaze. "This is way too much for me."

"Hell, I was punting. I didn't want you to know."

She touched his hot skin in the vee of his blue oxford shirt. "Didn't want me to know what?"

His breath hitched and quickened. Hunter's dizzying reaction to her touch set off a storm of sensations shooting through her.

"It's hard for a man to admit." He shook his head and his lower lip curled. "I want you. Only you."

Maddy could barely hear above her heart thwacking against her chest and in her ears.

His voice got rough and gravelly. "I see the way men look at you, how they harass you. I didn't want you to think of me as yet another horny guy. I wanted to be different for you. Crazy, huh?"

"No, I think it's sweet." She went up onto her tiptoes and pressed her lips to his full, hot mouth.

"No one has ever called me sweet." He held her face gently between his large hands while his thumbs rubbed over her eyebrows and down her cheeks to her lips. "You're sweet and delicious." He kissed her lips tentatively. "I want to make up for everything you've missed."

Maddy leaned in to his touch. Ice and heat danced along her skin as her mind absorbed Hunter's words. He wanted to take care of her, make up for her… Her stomach churned and her brain raced, trying to fathom Hunter's promises. Men made loads of pledges when they wanted sex, but apparently not Hunter. He was honest and honorable. And she wanted him. Only Hunter.

With his hard thighs pressing against her, she was having trouble concentrating on the words. Hunter sprinkled small kisses along her neck, making her melt against his rock-hard body. "You deserve to be treated like the very special woman you are. And I plan to shower you with attention and gifts."

The only gift she had wanted, he had already given her. The opal ring. And then, like a flash of summer lightning, she knew.

She pulled away from him. She needed to see his face. "My wedding ring?"

Hunter immediately stopped his crazy sensual assault. "You like it, don't you?"

She grasped Hunter's face and forced him to look at her. "Did you know?"

Hunter, the master of direct stares, had trouble looking her in the eye. "Yes, I read the report from your case worker."

In a split second, her lonely world was suddenly transformed into the dazzling aura of the profoundly new. He had understood how devastated she was when her only connection to her mother had been taken from her.

Maddy lifted her hand and touched the ring. Tears gathered behind her eyes. She swallowed hard and tried to find the words. "I can't believe it."

Hunter's face colored, and he cleared his throat.

"No one has ever cared." The tears started, not of sadness, but of joy and hopefulness.

Hunter kissed each tear on her face. "Oh, Maddy, don't cry. I can't stand to see you upset."

She laughed and giggled at the same time, delight bubbling up inside—so many emotions and so few words. Hunter had cared enough. "I'm never giving it back, Hunter."

He pulled her against him. "I never want you to give it back. I want the ring to be yours."

She wiped the tears from her cheeks. "My mother would've liked you."

"I'm sorry I never met your parents. They'd be so proud of the woman you've become."

Now the tears gushed down her face. How could she not love

this man? She threw herself ferociously against him, wrapping her arms around his neck to haul herself up against his lips. "I need you right now, Hunter Hines. It seems I'm having an over-the-top reaction to what an incredible man you are."

CHAPTER TEN

Maddy came at him like a woman in kick-ass karate mode. Like she always did, Maddy held nothing back. Hunter was man enough not to complain about an insane, passionate Maddy.

She kept slipping her little tongue into his mouth, sliding hers on his, then sucking on his. She took little bites along his neck, as if she was starved for him when he had been the one ravenous for her forever.

Like a train bearing down on him at full speed, she was on him, pressing and rubbing. Her enthusiasm made him senseless with need and love. He'd had sex with loads of women, but nothing compared to Maddy. She was honest and giving in her loving. He was never going to let her go.

He lifted her onto the countertop to slow down her uninhibited reaction. She had been willing for him to take her against the refrigerator door, but he wasn't about to treat Maddy so carelessly.

But with her tiny hands exploring, caressing his erection, his body tightened into massive lust.

He took her hands away, holding them between his, kissing her palms. "Maddy, I'm not going to last. I've been waiting a long time for you."

She took a shuddering breath when he licked her palm. Staring into her eyes, he tried to show what he felt for her. "I want to be gentle and tender like the man you deserve."

Maddy lunged forward, pressing her voluptuous chest against him. "After, Hunter…after…you can be gentle."

He laughed, a harsh sound. "You're killing me, sweetheart." But what a way to go.

Barely touching, he bent over and caressed her lips, teasing along the seam. Liking the way her breath froze and she waited, her body taut, he licked, nibbling as he unbuttoned her blouse.

When he had her blouse undone, Maddy thrust her chest forward, offering herself to him. And what a package. Her dusky nipples were erect and pushing against her lacy white bra. His heart hammered against his chest and his erection throbbed. Seeing Maddy unwrapped was too much. He needed her…against the refrigerator, on the counter…anywhere. Right goddamn now.

Maddy's breath hitched when he ran his knuckles down her chest. He had trouble catching his breath. "You're beautiful." He gently traced her breasts through her bra with his fingertip. "And you have beautiful breasts."

Maddy's face had reddened, and she breathed short, little pants through her open mouth. He slowly undid the front of her bra, releasing the soft, abundant flesh. Maddy might be petite, but she was one hell of a stacked woman.

Maddy gasped as he slowly explored her breasts with his fingertip. Maddy Jeffers, panting for his touch, was pushing him hard. He wanted to make it good for her, but he was torturing himself. "I've been waiting a long time to get my hands on you."

He lifted her breasts, gently squeezing, and then bent down and took one nipple into his mouth, circling it with his tongue.

"Ah!" Maddy fisted her hands into his hair, pulling him closer, holding him in place.

When he suckled her other breast, she threw back her head and squealed. No quiet woman, not his Maddy.

He was on fire for her. He caressed and played with her breasts while Maddy squirmed on the counter and then wrapped her legs around him tightly, bringing him into the cradle of her thighs. She brushed against his erection. Blinding lust shot through him and seared a burning path through his brain. He was fighting a losing battle with Maddy and her ferocious response to his touch.

He needed to be inside her. Sliding his hand under her skirt, his fingers wove their way to her womanly center. Maddy opened her legs, inviting him, and the blood rushed into his already throbbing groin.

He touched her moist, springy curls. The earthy female scent of her arousal demolished his control. He needed her now.

Her eyes drifted shut, and he could feel her quake on the edge of an orgasm. He thrust his tongue into her mouth as his finger sank into a hot, wet Maddy while she writhed, her hips twisting.

He put a second finger into her and took her nipple into his mouth, sucking hard. That was enough to send Maddy over the edge. With her head thrown back, she screamed his name. Her thighs quivered against his hands as she tightened and spasmed around his fingers.

Her body shuddered and collapsed, and she muttered, "I should've known you'd be masterful at this."

He pulled her against his chest, loving the feeling of her all relaxed and spineless against him. "You're one hell of a woman." A replete Maddy helped soften his driving hunger. He smoothed her tangled curls, then ran his hand down her back.

"That was fabulous," Maddy sighed.

His breath got rough and fast, and every last one of his lofty ideas of taking it slow and gentle were long gone. "I haven't even gotten started. That was a little warmup. Wait until I get you naked." Unable to not touch her, he kissed the top of her head, her closed eyelids, and her warm cheeks.

Her breathing evened and she seemed so relaxed he was worried she might have fallen asleep.

He lifted the lax Maddy against his chest and carried her into his bedroom. She was soft and satisfied; he was hard and in need. His body and muscles clenched as he looked down at her pale, voluptuous breasts. He took a slow breath, trying to get a handle on his dwindling control and his sprinting heart.

He stood close to the bed, careful not to disturb her as he leaned to gently place her on the bed. The urgency of his need to take her on a hard, long ride made his body burn.

Maddy sighed and tightened her arms around his neck, unwilling to release him. "Hunter, you are one helluva of a stud. I can't wait to undress you."

Every cell in his body and brain alerted into high-octane readiness. "I thought you were asleep."

"Asleep?" Maddy giggled as she rained wet kisses along his neck. "I was saving my strength to get you naked."

His mind went ballistic as his love and lust for this one woman exploded. He squeezed her against him. Her lemony scent, mixed with her feminine arousal, filled his mouth, his nose, his lungs, and surged into his groin. He had to taste her. He slowly lowered her to the floor and crushed her against his hard length.

Maddy melted against him, emitting a low purring sound. Strung tight, he started to hoist her up. Maddy gazed at him with heated eyes.

Holding her head steady with both hands, he used the tip of his tongue to tease her lips open. The small groan of pleasure at the back of her throat sent his pulse racing.

With her eyes closed, she sucked on his tongue while she trembled with broken, heavy breaths.

He needed her naked now—skin to skin, with her big, soft breasts crushed against him. He reached for the zipper on her skirt.

Maddy pushed his hands away. "It's my turn, Hunter. You had your turn in the kitchen." She reached for his shirt buttons, undoing each one slowly and carefully occasionally glancing up at him through her eyelashes with a wicked grin.

He gulped air, his pulse tripping. "I'm happy if we take

turns." He lifted her breasts and caressed the silky handful.

Maddy gasped and arched backward as he rolled her tight nipples between his fingertips.

She took a shuddering breath then pulled away. "Unfair, Hunter. It's still my turn." She reached for the last button on his shirt. He could feel her hot puffs of breath on his chest as she leaned to the task. "That woman had her hands on you, right here." She planted a love bite on his chest.

Shit, not what he wanted Maddy to be focused on now. "It doesn't matter," he rumbled.

"It matters." She bit him again. A soft bite that didn't hurt but sent sizzles of reaction along his nerve endings. Then she soothed it by licking his heated skin with her tiny tongue. "You belong to me."

Passion roared through him. He thought he knew what turned on meant. Until Maddy claimed him as her own, he'd had no idea.

She pulled his shirt off his arms while she trailed wet licks along his chest and abdomen. "She touched you here?" Each nip was followed by the tiny pink tongue. His erection twitched against the zipper, and he was in blissful agony. Until Maddy, he'd prided himself on having complete mastery of his body. She was going to be the death of him.

Maddy undid his belt, her knuckles rubbing against his abdomen and lower. "Did she touch you here?" She eased his zipper along his giant boner.

His brain was fried. Desperation for Maddy seized his entire body and soul. "I only want you."

Her petite hands were inside his boxers, squeezing him. Her voice was breathless. "You didn't answer the question."

His voice came out strangled. "What are you going to do if I say yes?"

A pink and glowing Maddy looked up, sexual heat glimmering in her eyes. "I'll soothe all the hurt with my lips and tongue."

As if he had taken a blow to his chest, his knees buckled.

Maddy's hands tightened on him.

He was on the verge of losing control. "Maddy, she didn't touch me. I never wanted anyone but you to touch me."

She bent over him, her hair brushing against his already rigid abdomen while she dragged his pants and boxers down. Now on her knees, she pulled his shoes off. She looked up, her blond hair all tussled, her eyes dancing with promise. "I'm glad I don't have to bite you, but I am still planning to kiss you all over."

A masterful Maddy at his knees pushed him over the edge. "Honey, I can't take any more." He kicked off his shoes, pants, and boxers and pulled her up into his arms. He tugged at her skirt, pulling it down as Maddy stepped out. She had the tiniest wisp of nude lace over her blond curls. Gone beyond gentleness, he ground desperately against her while he kneaded her soft, rounded cheeks.

Maddy's fingers clutched his back. "I need you now, Hunter."

He got rid of her thong and then laid her on the bed.

Maddy—all pink, her damp hair clinging to her temples, her soft breasts with their dusky nipples erect—inflamed him. She was perfect and she was his. Only his.

"Hunter, you're so…" She swallowed hard as she stared at his erection. "More than I could ever have imagined." She opened her arms to him.

He grabbed a condom from the bedside stand, his hands shaking as he rolled it on. He wasn't sure if it was the hunger for Maddy that was riding him so hard or the way she watched, her big blue eyes wide, but there was only so much a man could take. He had never experienced such an uproar of love and need.

He levered himself, keeping his weight in his elbows, rubbing his chest over her luscious breasts. She gasped at the brush of his heated skin. He could barely breathe from the pleasure of touching Maddy. He took her mouth, devouring her, as he nudged against her wet tightness. He sucked on her skin—her neck and behind her ear—making her thrash under him. He bent and took her breasts into his mouth, pulling hard on her nipple. Maddy squirmed and her nails dug into his shoulders.

He slid his arms under her thighs and thrust deep inside. He wanted to thrust into her again and again, but forced himself to stay still until she could accommodate his large size.

Maddy pleaded, "Now, Hunter. I can't wait any longer."

He looked down at her face, at her eyes bright with passion and her lips open, panting. She moved against him, setting a fast pace, her hands grabbing, coaxing him on. She demanded he stroke harder, sending him deeper.

Her breaths came quicker, hotter as he tugged hard on her breast. He lifted her hips higher and pumped to give her more friction. With him buried deep, he felt the grip of her body. She groaned and then screamed his name as she rushed headlong into orgasm.

His thrust one last time and let the wave of Maddy's after-spasms take him. And like Maddy, he threw back his head and shouted his release. Never in his life had he shouted. Never in his life had he ever lost control. Never in his life had he fully loved a woman.

Hunter woke with Maddy curled close to his side. She had one leg over his groin, and her arm was across his chest, near his heart. He could feel her small, snuffling snores on his chest. Her blond curls were awry. He bent his head to get a whiff of her lemon shampoo and the scent of Maddy. He didn't want to wake her. He didn't want this first night with her to end. Like the dedicated Marine she was, she had focused and given a hundred percent.

He wanted to take her again, but she was most likely sore. He was a big man, and they had been insatiable. He lightly ran his hand along the soft dip in her waist to her hip. Maddy stirred and reached for him.

He wasn't sure if she'd understood when he told her he wanted her to have the ring forever…he meant marriage.

CHAPTER ELEVEN

The next morning, Maddy stood at the classroom door waiting for the women to arrive. She was dressed in the same outfit—long-sleeve blouse, black skirt, ballet flats—prepared to discuss American meal planning and preparation. She couldn't suppress the big smile that broke out every time she thought about her passionate night with Hunter. He had dedicated the entire night to pleasuring her. And he knew how to slowly drive a woman out of her mind. Her sensual reverie was interrupted by the sounds of acrimonious, muffled voices.

The intensity of the argument escalated until it echoed in the empty hallway, so Maddy wandered out of the classroom to investigate. Guli and Rasa were standing close to each other, and Guli was speaking quickly in a harsh voice, her intonation and sharp gestures telling Maddy the older woman was angry. Rasa shook her head and started to walk away. Guli grabbed her arm and fiercely pointed in the young woman's face. Maddy heard Guli screech: "Kaafar—infidel."

Maddy stepped back into the classroom before the women noticed her. Only nonbelievers were called infidels. What had Rasa done to deserve such an offensive insult? Was it because she didn't wear a burka?

Maddy plastered a smile on her face and waited at the door to greet the angry women. Rasa arrived first, and Maddy could see the tears pooling in her eyes. Maddy welcomed her, and Rasa nodded and went to sit in the circle of chairs. Neither Guli nor

Sadia came into the classroom until class had begun. Obviously, they didn't want to be greeted by an American infidel. Their attendance in this class didn't add up…unless Abu had required them to attend.

After the hour, Maddy walked to her desk, pleased with how the class had gone despite the stormy beginning. Of course, Guli and Sadia offered nothing when she asked the women to discuss their family's favorite recipe. Rasa, who sat on the other side of the room from Guli and Sadia, remained subdued, with no smiles or jokes for her friends.

Maddy was excited to get Hunter's take on the argument and what it might mean. She wanted to discuss other strategies to engage the Hamman women.

Who was she kidding? She was plain excited to see Hunter. She had never felt this way about anyone. Did he miss her the way she missed him?

Maddy started to stack up the pictures of American foods she had displayed during the class after the women left. A moment later, Rasa came back into the classroom.

Rasa smiled tentatively and walked toward the desk. "Do you have plans for this afternoon?" The little hairs on Maddy's arms prickled in awareness. Did the argument with Guli have anything to do with this sudden interest in Maddy's afternoon? Was Maddy the infidel Guli had referred to?

Rasa's eyes gave nothing away, and, because she wore a niqab, Maddy couldn't read any changes in her facial expressions.

"Cirus loved playing with you at the market, and you like babies so much. I thought you might enjoy visiting with me and Cirus this afternoon."

This was the problem with their line of work—everyone was a suspect. Including an outgoing mother with an adorable baby boy.

"I'd be delighted to come to your home some another afternoon. Maybe next week?"

Rasa's eyes darkened. "You cannot come today?"

"No, I've already made plans." She certainly wouldn't go into specifics—that she planned on seducing her pretend husband after making him dinner. She might not know how to cook, but she, too, could grill steak and make a salad. Based on the way Hunter had responded to her taking her clothes off, she wasn't sure when they'd get to dinner anyway. She definitely had plans.

The woman shifted her weight and fingered her veil. Her sudden nervousness alerted Maddy. "Are you worried about Cirus?" Maddy had learned from her time in Afghanistan that she always learned more by asking about a woman's child instead of asking direct questions—like why were you and Guli arguing? She couldn't let this opportunity to learn more about Abu's family slip by. Did Rasa hope to talk to her about the argument?

"Yes, he has a rash, and I hoped you could look at it."

Truly concerned, Maddy came around the desk. "Is he sick? Have a fever?"

"I don't think so, but he is hot. Maybe just the heat, but you know how a mother worries. I only live a block from here. Could you please come over for a minute to look at his rash?"

Maddy nodded. If Rasa took Cirus to the clinic, it could take hours. "I will walk with you and take a quick peek at Cirus." She didn't believe anything could be wrong with the happy, healthy toddler she had played with yesterday, but here was an excuse to discuss other, more intriguing matters.

Maddy was now in a rush to get home. Home. She liked the idea of a home with Hunter. She hurried down Rainier Avenue, her skirt swinging back and forth. She was an hour late after her stop to see Cirus. The baby had a little heat rash on his neck, nothing alarming. The visit had taken longer than she'd hoped since all the social niceties had to be observed. Unfortunately, Rasa disclosed nothing about the argument.

Maddy hesitated to believe subterfuge was involved in Rasa's request, but she did want to discuss the whole episode with Hunter. Her first priority was resuming where they had left off last night, but tonight, she planned to do the seducing. Then she'd snuggle against his hard chest, and like a married couple, discuss the day. The thought made her impatient and eager as she waited for the light to change.

She had texted Hunter when she left Rasa's house, but he hadn't responded. Why wouldn't he respond? Above everything else, Hunter was reliable.

She had also stopped to buy steaks at Halal Meats, the butcher shop right next door to Abu's restaurant. She decided to do a bit of reconnaissance in her role as a wife shopping for dinner. She had asked innocently if the butcher had eaten at the restaurant. The man was very polite. He told her he supplied the meat for the restaurant, smiled…and that was the end of the conversation. She had failed at investigating today, but she was confidant she'd excel in her role as Hunter's wife tonight.

She hurried up the front porch steps, ready to throw herself into his arms. She didn't think of Hunter as a demonstrative man, but after last night, she realized the careful man was ready to express a lot of stored-up, passionate feelings, and she was delighted to be the recipient. She turned the knob, but the door was locked. Where had Hunter gone, and why hadn't he texted? Did he have a surprise planned?

Maddy dug into her shoulder bag for the key. She opened the door and yelled. "Hunter, I'm home." Her voice came out breathless, as if she had run home.

No answer. She walked to the sparkling kitchen. Hunter had cleaned. She strode back to their bedroom. Hunter had tidied the entire room, her clothes, thrown on the floor last night in wanton abandon, were now folded on the neatly made-up bed.

Nothing looked out of place. She went back to the dining

room to see if Hunter had left her a note like a real husband might do.

Nothing. A light shiver bristled down her neck and spine. Having worked with Hunter on their last assignment, she knew he was a stickler for staying in communication. Something didn't feel right. But after last night, her whole perception of Hunter had been turned upside down and sideways. He had been right that their relationship changed her perspective about the assignment.

She texted him again. If he had been out running errands, he'd have given her a heads-up.

She carried the steaks to the refrigerator, and a rush of warm emotions came over her, remembering Hunter lifting her onto the counter. The way she had pressed against him, her legs wrapped around him, his stubble had abraded her neck in the most scintillating way. She needed to get her act together. But intimacy with a caring man was new to her.

She'd give Hunter a half hour, and then she'd call Forret from the burner phone. If Hunter was delayed, he'd be pissed she made the connection with their handler, but if the roles were reversed, he would definitely follow protocol.

She walked to their bedroom to change out of her hot clothes. The man had almost an obsession about orderliness. Growing up with a Marine father, Hunter probably never knew any different. She'd try to pick up to please him, but she was not a tidy person about anything, so they both would have to adjust. She liked the idea of bringing a little bit of chaos into Hunter's controlled world.

She peeled out of her long skirt and wondered how the Afghan women could stand being covered up all the time. Like Hunter's strict orderliness, the women had never experienced the freedom of having the cool air caress their bare skin and couldn't possibly know what they were missing.

After changing into shorts and a tank top, Maddy decided she would look at the surveillance tapes Hunter had been watching this morning before she alerted Forret. Maybe Hunter had seen something. It still didn't explain his lack of communication, though.

She sat at the desk and turned on the multiple screens monitoring Abu's apartment. There were cameras monitoring the parking lot, the entrance, and the hall outside their apartment.

Maddy checked each screen. A short Asian man parked his beat-up Honda Civic and walked toward the six-story, remodeled apartment building. Maddy reached to scroll back for earlier tapes when motion on the screen monitoring the entrance caught her eye.

Rasa, with baby Cirus, was walking into the building. Rasa had told her she planned to put Cirus down for his nap as soon as Maddy left her apartment. Maddy's entire being went on hyper-alert focus. Her muscles constricted, and her brain narrowed into single-minded concentration.

She watched the screen as Rasa walked through the front door of the apartment complex, waiting to see if she would enter the Hammans' hall. Since their apartment was on the ground floor, she didn't have to wait long before she saw Rasa walk down the narrow corridor. Maddy's suspicion grew exponentially when the woman kept peering over her shoulder as if she knew Maddy was watching her.

Sadia opened the door for Rasa, who hurried into the apartment. Maddy's heart punched hard against her chest. What the hell was going on? During his surveillance, had Hunter seen something at the apartment?

Maddy kept her eye on the monitor, tracking the Hammans' front door as she simultaneously scrolled through the earlier tapes from the other cameras. Like a hammer kick delivered to the chest, her body bolted backward at seeing Hunter walking next to Sadia into the apartment complex. Maddy assumed it was Sadia from the way she moved, but she couldn't be a hundred percent sure because of her burka.

Confounded by the sight, she replayed the moment over and over. Her brain sped as her muscles knotted into a tight fist of fear and anxiety. Hunter marched next to the woman like a Marine, his shoulders back, chin thrust forward, spine and neck rigid. He went willingly to the apartment, but he was in fighting mode. Sadia was no threat to him, so what did he expect to encounter that had him wound up into battle mode?

Maddy quickly went through the tape monitoring the apartment door. Her hands were shaking as she scrolled through the recording. Maddy watched Guli open the door and say something to Hunter, who rushed into the apartment.

Maddy felt something black and frightening skitter up her spine. She tried to logically recount the possible reasons Hunter might have gone to the apartment. Nothing made any sense.

She shouldn't be worried for his safety since she knew he could easily disarm two women, one of them old. But uneasiness still tugged at her chest, and fear was inching its way into her mind when she considered the possibility that it had been a setup to draw him into the apartment for Abu and his men. Hunter was an experienced military agent—he would have assessed the threat.

Was there a more innocent reason? She'd like to believe it was innocent, but she read Hunter's body language. He had gone into the apartment expecting trouble. She would have known if he had called for backup, wouldn't she?

Maddy went to the locked safe and got out her Glock and one of the many burner cell phones stored there. She noted that Hunter's Glock was gone. She dialed Forret while she continued to watch the monitors for any further movement from the apartment.

Her breathing quickened into aggressive surges. Her body was pulsing with adrenaline, like a caffeine rush from too many espressos. She recognized the rush—the sweaty palms, the rapid breaths, the racing heart. She was ready to take down whatever shit Hunter had gotten himself into. Taking slow, measured breaths and willing her body to relax, she cracked her neck, trying to relax the taut neck muscles as she waited for Forret to pick up.

"Forret," came the imperious voice of Homeland Security.

"Forret, this is Jeffers. We might have a situation."

"Might have. What the hell does that mean?"

She was going to kill Hunter for this phone call once she saved his sorry ass. Why had he broken protocol and gone into the apartment alone? "I have Hunter on the surveillance tape going into the Hammans' apartment with Abu's sister, Sadia. According to the time on the tape, he's been in there a half hour."

"Go on." Forret's voice was calm now, but she knew he was preparing himself for the worst.

"He isn't answering his phone and he's taken his Glock."

"Where were you while he decided to act like the Lone Ranger?"

"I was at class and then delayed by one of my students."

"Do you have any idea why Hines would do this?"

"No, but by the way he's moving on the tape, I'd say he was suspicious of the situation."

"You're supposed to be the one making contact with the women. It makes no sense. These are observant women who don't speak to men. Why is he there?"

"Look, if I knew, I wouldn't have called you. I thought you might know." Maddy was now getting pissed. It was time to act.

"He's your partner, and you're calling me? I should never have okayed you two for this assignment."

A slow burn of rage was working its way up her body and about to blow out the top of her head.

"Forret, I'm going into the apartment. And you need to put the team on alert. And despite your asshole attitude, Hunter is a top-notch agent. Just do your job. Give me backup." She ended the call and stormed out of the house.

CHAPTER TWELVE

His first sensation was a razor-sharp pain drilling into the back of his skull. The second was an overwhelming urge to barf up his guts. Disoriented and in agony, Hunter got one eye open. The silent darkness and an overpowering resiny, spicy smell hit him smack in the face. Acid bile rose into his throat, and he gulped against the involuntary spasms.

He closed his eyes and panted through his mouth, willing his body to cooperate. The pungent smells were familiar. Cinnamon and cardamom. Was he back in Afghanistan?

Wanting to fade back into oblivion, he closed his eyes for a brief second. Maddy. His brain jolted wide awake. Where was she? Panic pumped through him. Had they gotten to her? He tried to push to an upright position, but not only were his hands and feet tied, he was also wrapped in something, immobile. From the rough feel against his face and the overwhelming smell of Afghan spices, he surmised that he was wrapped in a dining carpet from Afghanistan.

A rush of faded memories flashed through him in seconds. He had been suspicious when Abu's sister had appeared at their house, maintaining that a feverish Maddy was vomiting in their apartment. It was a simple ploy, but it had worked—not because he completely accepted the story, but because if they had captured Maddy, he had to rescue her. And he hadn't been willing to delay because, in either scenario, Maddy needed him. He'd rushed over to the apartment.

He couldn't move his hand to touch the back of his skull, but he recognized the excruciating throbbing pain of a blunt force injury. Hadn't he learned anything from his time in Afghanistan? The women could be as fierce as the men. What choice had there been? Maddy was either ill or held hostage. Despite his painful injuries, he still would risk his own safety to rescue Maddy.

He had to get out of here, wherever here was, and find her. She didn't suspect that the mother and the sister were working with Abu. Did they already have her? He couldn't allow any thoughts to distract his purpose. One step at a time.

His skull pain and the need to blow his guts were a distraction, but his years of discipline and training kicked him into focus. He brushed his back against the floor, feeling for his gun. They had taken his Glock.

He didn't know if he had enough space, but he was going to get out of this damn rug and then deal with the next problem of his shackled hands and feet.

Hunter stiffened his spine and neck and shoved his shoulder forward as hard as he could to roll over. Because his feet were tied together, he had to exert a huge effort to accomplish the smallest awkward progress. He threw himself against the floor. He sucked into the hurt as he rolled flat on his face, pressing into the musty smell with the wool fibers brushing against his nose and lips. He couldn't be sure this effort wasn't futile. His next move, going from his stomach to his back, was more difficult and required more focused coordination than brute strength. He scrunched his feet and knees up to lever the weight of his legs and hips and flipped.

Visions of Maddy needing him kept his concentration sharp and him oblivious to the background noise of a piercing headache and nausea. Nothing equaled the tangle of his emotions and fears for Maddy right now. Nothing. The mission where he had been stabbed and left for dead in the Registan desert didn't come close to the terror gripping him now.

His gyrations told him he was in a larger space than the apartment where he had been whacked. Had they driven him away from the complex? Was he rolled in a carpet to cover their exit from the apartment building?

The final push exacerbated his headache until the pain reverberated in his ears. This last roll left him facedown again, but he was free of the confines of the rug. He quickly rolled to his back, sat up, and checked out the space. He was in a small storage room, about twenty-five square feet, in a damp basement. There were two small windows, neither big enough to allow him to escape. The floor and walls were cement, and on one wall there were computer screens and an array of tech gear—a hell of a lot more than he and Maddy had from the FBI. The enemies were tech rich and violent.

He definitely didn't have much time to make his escape if they'd left him in the center of their operation. The deduction was simple: They planned to kill him. He had to get the hell out of here and find Maddy.

He'd have been screwed if they had tied his hands to his feet. Now all he had to do was get his Mule knife out of his shoe. Not an easy trick, but one he had mastered a long time ago. Snapping the locking mechanism on zip ties was Survival 101 for a field agent.

He raised his arms above his head, anticipating that it was going to hurt like a son of a bitch. He jerked his hands down— fast, with all his might, with his elbow angled back to the point of pain. His size gave him incredible advantage for leverage. He struck his tied wrists against his tightened upper abdomen and the tie broke apart on his first try, although his wrists hurt like a mother, and his head and gut were spinning from the fast movement.

He bent over to reach into his tennis shoe for his folding knife. Grateful they hadn't discovered it, he made quick work of the ankle ties by sawing through them. He jumped to his feet.

The two windows were still a no-go. The door was thick but

had only one lock. He listened at the door and heard nothing. Whatever they were planning to do with him, they were sure to be back soon.

He dug into his pants pocket where he kept his Bogota mini-picks. As his father always said, "No Marine ever goes unprepared." He used his picks quickly. The sound of the lock opening resounded in the silence and in his pounding head. He quietly placed his Bogota back in his pocket and opened his knife, ready to disarm anyone who got in his way.

Slowly, he opened the door and scanned the long cement-and-cinderblock hall. No one was in the immediate area. He slid along the wall, every sense heightened, muscles clenched, ready to strike.

He encountered no one, reaching the cement steps leading out without incident. No sound came from above. He took the twelve steps to the main floor. By the cheapness and period of the construction, he surmised he was in the basement of the Graham Place apartments where Abu and his family lived. He pushed the heavy fire door open to the lobby of the apartment complex that promised a "secure, gated community." "Gated" turned out to be a two-foot-high wrought iron fence surrounding the hundred-unit building, and security was nonexistent.

He scanned the lobby. No one in sight.

They had taken his phone, so no way to call for backup. He needed to get into the apartment to find out if Maddy was in danger.

Turning right, he headed back to the Hamman apartment. He stood outside the door and listened. Thanks to shitty workmanship, he could hear through the pressboard door.

He strained to hear the voices. His heart skipped a beat when he heard Maddy's voice. She was alive, and she sounded like she was fighting mad. Relief and joy shot through him. He hadn't allowed himself any thought other than to make sure she was safe and secure. Now he was ready to go in and save his woman.

He carefully turned the doorknob with one hand, gripping his knife in the other. Maddy stood with her back to him, but, even with his best stealth, she whirled around and pointed her Glock at him.

"Oh my God, Hunter. Thank God." Her voice was wobbly, and he would've sworn her face contorted as if she might cry. She quickly turned back toward the sobbing Rasa, who was clinging to her toddler. Not the time for a happy reunion. Unlike him, Maddy had learned vigilance from her time in Afghanistan.

And at this moment, he hated his work—that a loving mother wanted to create chaos and violence. Weren't mothers supposed to want a safer, more peaceful world for their children? What the hell did he know? His mother had deserted him.

He walked over to stand beside Maddy. "Where's Abu?"

"That's what I'm trying to find out." She looked into his eyes with the most honest look of love and need, and he had to stifle the urge to haul her into his arms and kiss her silly.

"Okay, but maybe we should get out of here, since we don't know who is coming back."

Rasa stuttered. "They're gone. I was supposed to distract you until they got away."

Never moving the pointed gun, Maddy dug into the pocket of her skirt and threw him a burner phone. "Why don't you call Forret? The team is on standby."

Maddy turned back to the woman. God, he loved a take-charge woman. She was his perfect counterpart.

He would never admit that once he knew she was safe, he was happy to let the cavalry take over. His head was pounding, he had a bit of double vision, and from the way his legs shook, the effort he'd expended in his escape was catching up with him.

Maddy stepped closer to the woman, who trembled visibly. The toddler grinned and reached out his arms for Maddy.

Maddy's voice was clipped. "You were supposed to keep me away to lure Hunter to the apartment, right? That was the whole bullshit about Cirus's rash? So they could take Hunter prisoner?"

Maddy turned back and scanned his body. "Are you hurt from your escape?" He liked that she already gave him credit for escaping. Never hurts a man's ego when his woman recognizes his skill.

"Never felt better. How about you?"

She inspected his face very carefully. "Good, I'm good."

He hit the emergency code on the phone. The team would be here in less than five minutes. "Let's take her outside and wait for the team."

"Bad memories from this apartment?" Maddy's sassiness was helping to revive him.

He smiled at her. "No, just don't want to get trapped with only one gun and a knife between us."

"A gun, two knives, and two pissed off Marines. That's enough, dontcha think?"

He laughed out loud. "You're right, my Mad Marine."

"Clever, Hunter." She pointed the gun back at the woman. "Start walking. Where is Abu? And what's his plan?"

"Abu isn't involved. Guli is in charge. She recognized your husband from TV. She knew he was in the American military and believed you were on to her and Sadia."

Maddy shook her head. "Not believing it. Where is Abu?"

"You have to believe me. Guli is in charge. Abu knows nothing about his mom. He's a good man."

Hunter opened the door and checked the hall before signaling them to come.

Maddy walked behind Rasa and Cirus. "Keep talking."

"I'm one of the many women she uses. She said she would kill my mother in Afghanistan if I didn't do what she said. She shows us videos of our families in our country and threatens to kill them if we don't help her." Rasa turned and faced Maddy. "I'd never hurt you. Please believe me." The woman cried. "You've been so kind to me and Cirus."

Hunter stepped forward to intimidate the woman. "How will

an old woman in the States hurt your family in Afghanistan?"

"Sadia's husband is in our country. He is part of it all."

Maddy wasn't swayed from her duty by Cirus's toothy smiles. Her gun was steady and pointed at his mother. "All?"

"Guli and Sadia are here to recruit our women for ISIS. Her brother in Jakarta is also involved."

"Where are Guli and Sadia headed?"

"I don't know. Maybe Jakarta or back to our country."

CHAPTER THIRTEEN

By the time they had moved outside to the parking lot, a representative from every intelligence agency in the Northwest had arrived. SWAT teams surrounded the building. Black vans blocked every exit from the apartment complex. A helicopter hovered overhead. Darney, in his FBI Kevlar vest, stood in the middle of the storm, directing the action.

Forret, dressed in full combat gear, with a Glock 40 in hand and a Remington 700 and stun baton on his utility belt, ran toward them. Three team members surrounded them. Forret quickly inspected each person. He kept his eyes on Hunter. "Are you okay?"

Maddy lowered her gun. "Abu's mother and sister are part of it." Maddy pointed at Rasa. "She was threatened that if she didn't help them take out me and Hunter her family would be hurt. I don't believe she's part of the bigger plot."

With their guns still pointed at Rasa, the officers escorted the mother and child to a van. Maddy followed. At the van, Maddy leaned over and spoke softly to a terrified Rasa and stroked Cirus's head.

Hunter quickly updated Forret about the mother and sister's trap, the highly sophisticated equipment in the basement, and Rasa's information about the ISIS connection.

A charged-up Forret spoke into a radio in a clipped and precise voice, directing the operation to the basement and the Hammans' apartment.

Hunter said, "I'd put an APB out on the mother, daughter, and Abu. I'm sure they're trying to get on a plane or ferry out of here right now."

"Already done," Forret replied.

Hunter tracked Maddy through the throng of men. She was now reporting to Darney, as he had done with Forret. Darney was definitely close to Maddy, too close. And judging by the animation on Darney's face and the way he smiled at Maddy, the man was impressed.

Despite his headache throbbing from the deafening sounds of the helicopter and the fast-paced action around him, Hunter wanted to get close to Darney and explain a few salient facts.

The only thing holding him back was Maddy's reaction. She was a Marine doing her job, and if he did his caveman stuff, she'd be pissed. But he had been beat over the head, tied up, and bundled up like a California sushi roll, and during that entire time, his focus had been only on saving Maddy. He was usually a patient man, but not with her. Not today. He needed his Maddy to comfort and love.

Forret stuck his phone into his pocket "Man, you're pathetic."

Hunter stiffened. He thought he was doing a damn good job of hiding his concussion. He knew the symptoms, and he'd put himself at a Grade 2 concussion, but since he didn't know how long he had been out, possibly Grade 3. Didn't matter, it hurt like a son of a bitch.

"The colonel was right about you two. You'll make a good team now that you've worked out your feelings."

Despite the sensation of buffalos stampeding through his head, he could possibly manage to hurt Forret. "What's with the psychobabble shit? This job too much for you?"

Forret's eyes darted back and forth on the movement of his troops, but his mouth curved into a smirk. He nodded to someone behind Hunter. "I'm a trained observer. You couldn't have been any more obvious about your feelings for Jeffers. It was very entertaining to watch your reaction when I suggested I'd partner with her. And it looks like she has gotten over her objections to you as her husband."

Hunter followed Forret's gaze. Maddy kept turning back and checking on him. She smiled then continued to talk with Darney. His headache and Forret's bullshit disappeared in the sunlight of Maddy's attention.

Forret snickered. "Nothing more you can do here. Go get some rest. You look like shit."

"Go to hell, Forret."

Maddy gave Darney a full debriefing, but she was anxious to have Hunter assessed. It was obvious he had suffered a head injury. And the big, macho man was going to deny that he needed any help.

Forret walked past her. "Good work, Jeffers. Get Hines some medical care."

"My next priority, sir." Maddy pulled herself up into her full height of five feet and tucked her chin. Getting Hunter to accept medical care was going to be as hard as pointing a gun at sweet Cirus. Sometimes the job sucked and made you wonder what kind of war you were fighting.

"They've got Abu. He was walking down the street," Forret suddenly shouted.

An agitated Abu was led to the parking lot by two agents. His hands were tied behind his back, his eyes wide with shock, and he kept shouting in Dari. "Where is my mother, my sister?"

Maddy walked over to Hunter. "Go sit down. I'm going to translate for Forret."

He shook his head. "I can translate for them. Besides, Abu speaks English."

"I'll get more information if I speak to him in his language when he's upset."

Hunter's face was pale and his pupils looked equal, but he was good at masking his pain.

"Go sit down before you fall down." Maddy tried to give him a badass stare, but she realized it wasn't working when he grinned back at her. "If you don't sit down, I'll call an ambulance and make a very big deal about your head injury."

"If I sit down, will you promise to take me home? No hospital."

"Only if you tell me the truth about Las Vegas."

"Las Vegas?"

"Were you really offered a job as a comedian?"

Hunter rolled his eyes upward. "You want to know about that now?"

"Yes. While I have you in my power." She ran her hand along his bulging bicep. After the terrible day spent believing Hunter had been captured and possibly killed, all she wanted to do was to take him home. And for the first time in her life, she could admit that she needed a man's comfort. Not any man. Hunter.

He stepped closer, crowding her. "How unfair to take advantage of an injured man, but damn sexy. I did do stand-up comedy but was never offered a professional gig. Are you disappointed?"

"Never. I could never be disappointed in you. I'll take you home first, but no promises about the hospital until I thoroughly assess your injury."

Hunter gave her the sweetest, most besotted look. "I like a take-charge woman."

Maddy wanted to rush into his arms and spill out all the fears she'd suffered, worrying that Abu had killed him.

Abu's wretched cry interrupted. "No, no. I'm innocent."

She pointed Hunter toward the open FBI van. "Go sit down."

He rolled his eyes. "Whatever you say, honey." Maddy didn't

believe his nonchalant act for a minute. For Hunter to forego control, he must be really hurting.

Maddy hurried over to Forret and Darney and the ten men surrounding Abu. She had told Darney that Rasa insisted Abu was not part of the terrorism plot. Maddy wanted to believe what Rasa said. And the fact that Abu came back to the apartment complex when his mother and sister had fled made it more likely he wasn't part of the plan.

By the rigid stances of the FBI and Homeland Security agents, they weren't as willing to buy Abu's innocence.

When Abu saw her, his eyes brightened. "Mrs. Grady, please tell them. I'm not a terrorist. You know my mother, my sister. I own a restaurant."

Maddy spoke in Dari. "Everything you say is true. Where are your mother and sister?"

Abu answered in English and spoke to the men. "My mother and sister are in the apartment, getting our dinner ready."

An impatient Forret said, "Your mother and sister attacked our agent, tied him up, and left him in the basement where they have a tech center. Who else is working with you?"

"No, no. I don't believe it. They would never dishonor my father's memory." Abu grabbed his heart. "His dream was to have us be free."

Forret shook his head. "Get him out of here."

"Please, we came to America to get away from the hatred, the violence. We are good people."

Maddy watched as they put Abu in the van and drove away. Rasa and Cirus had already been taken away to be questioned. The FBI had taken over the investigation, and the FBI cyber team would spend hours in the basement with what Hunter described as their tech center.

Hunter and Maddy had done their part.

It was time for her to take care of Hunter. He sat on the back of the SUV, looking tired and rumpled, her protector and dragon slayer with a few raw wounds. But she would make it up to him.

She had lots of feelings stored up and ready to spend on loving Hunter.

Butterflies fluttered in her stomach at the thought of home. She was impatient to take Hunter home. Not just a stop, but a home.

She had to stand on tiptoe to reach his injury. She felt for the contusion on the back of his head. It was at least four inches by four inches and swelling. "How is your headache?"

"Not bad."

"That bad, huh? We've got to get ice on it to bring the swelling down and get you a CT scan. Are your symptoms Grade 2 or 3?"

"All of the above, but I'm not going to the hospital. I know exactly what I need, and it isn't a CT scan."

"What if you're bleeding internally?"

"Trust me. I'm not."

"And how would you know?" She put her hands on her hips. "Are you having memory problems?"

"No. I remember exactly what you looked like when you screamed my name last night."

Maddy felt the heat burning the tops of her ears.

"And the way you—"

Maddy put her hand over his mouth, looking around. He licked her palm. She pulled her hand back.

"Okay, obviously your headache isn't that bad." She took his arm and tried to help him out of the van. "We'll decide later if you need a CT scan."

He stood and leaned down near her ear. His hot breath whispered across her face. "Later sounds perfect.'

"Stop it. Seriously, Hunter, what do you need? Don't be all macho and on the make. They bashed you on the head."

"I need you, Tylenol, and ice. In that order. Take me home, Maddy."

"Home?"

"We only live two houses away. I would like to lie down." Hunter did a pretend leer, waggling his eyebrows.

"For a man who suffered a major blow to his head, you're sure acting energetic."

"Come on, Maddy. You know I'm fine. All they'd do at the hospital is observe me. You can observe me at home. Take me home."

Suddenly, it hit her that their assignment was finished. "We're finished. We don't have a home."

"Yeah, we do." Not caring whether anyone was watching. Hunter pulled her into his arms. "Wherever you are is home for me."

"But…"

"We'll find us a real home and be a real husband and wife."

EPILOGUE

Half asleep, Maddy reached across the pillow for Hunter but came up empty. She rolled over and sat up, naked. She couldn't suppress her grin, remembering how Hunter wouldn't lie down and rest unless she got naked and in bed with him.

When she hadn't been snuggled against the wounded man, she had monitored his mental status. And in the early dawn, a very lusty Hunter had woken her and made tender, gentle love. She had cried after their lovemaking. The feelings of being cherished and loving fiercely were all new, tilting her in a disorienting way.

She stretched. It was time to face the real world. Right when she was about to go in search of her pretend husband, he appeared with a tray stacked with coffee, muffins, and the fruit they had bought at the market.

It wasn't fair that she was still naked in bed and Hunter was dressed. She wanted him to lose his clothes and get back in bed. She wasn't ready for the demands of the day to creep into their wonderful interlude.

Since Hunter was dressed in his standard oxford shirt and slacks, she pulled the covers up to her neck. His eyes were bright and intense, warming her from the inside out. He leaned down and kissed her, a sweet, tender touch that grew into hot possession. When he stopped, she realized he had pulled down the sheet. "I like seeing you, Maddy. Don't cover up."

He wanted her again. She could tell by the way his breath

quickened and his eyes darkened. This man had been so caring and gentle last night, and insatiable despite his injury.

"You should be in bed. I'm not the patient."

He sat the tray down on the bed. "Having my wife in my bed cured me."

Maddy scanned his face as he unfolded a napkin and placed it on her lap, his knuckles brushing her breast. His dark stubble was gone, and his inky black hair was combed back away from his angular face. Amazingly, there were no obvious signs of what he had suffered yesterday. The handsome man looked robust, his olive skin glowing and his dark eyes gleaming.

And when he smiled, his angles softened and relaxed. "Remember when you told me your husband would serve you in bed?"

He sat on the bed, poured coffee, and handed the mug to her. "Here is your coffee, exactly as you like it—dark, with no cream or sugar. Served to you by your grateful husband."

Maddy took a greedy sip of the piping hot brew, in need of caffeine and grateful for a distraction from her jumbled, intense emotions. And feeling a little unsure after her outpouring of love in the desperate throes of passion. "Thank you."

"No, thank you for taking care of me last night. I've never had such loving attention." Hunter's cheeks flushed. His voice got rough with emotion. "Maddy, I want to marry you as soon as you're ready. We'll have to report in, but we're both up for a furlough."

Maddy moaned. "Oh, shit. We've got to report in." She searched the room for her phone. "What time is it?"

"I already checked in with Forret for both of us. I explained how you were up all night watching for signs of concussion. Forret might as well have laughed in my face. He's on to us, and it seems the colonel has been, too."

Maddy felt the heat moving up her face. "The colonel? Why? What did Forret say?"

"He said I'd be a fool not to marry you right away since there are men lined up, wanting you."

Maddy giggled. "He did not."

"No, but he did say they have Guli and Sadia in custody. They were trying to board a flight to L.A. connecting to Jakarta, where Guli's brother lives. Guli embraced her brother's radical ways after her husband's death. She holds Americans responsible and wants revenge. Sadia and her husband are part of the network, but Guli was the one in charge of recruiting the young, displaced women for ISIS. Sadia was the tech specialist who sent embedded, subversive emails to the women she befriended in the class."

"Oh my God. That is unbelievable. What happened to Rasa and Abu?"

"Rasa and Cirus were released, but Abu is still in custody. They are checking everything before they release him, but Forret said they don't have any evidence connecting him to his mother and sister's activities. They are going through his computers and email. The email to Brandon Billow was from his sister, not Abu."

"How very sad. Guli destroyed her family with her hatred and need for revenge."

"Forget them. Back to my question."

Maddy lifted her eyebrows. "I don't recall hearing a question."

Hunter took her left hand into his. The opal glimmered all the colors of a rainbow. "Maddy, please say you'll marry me. I love you."

And in that moment, Maddy chose love and hope over audacity and fear. "I love you, Hunter Hines. Any man who is willing to go into harm's way for me must be a man in love."

"I'd risk everything for you, Maddy."

"Me, too, Hunter. You're a risk I can't resist."

BONUS CONTENT

A CHRISTMAS WEDDING CEREMONY

BY JACKI DELECKI

CHAPTER ONE

Maddy crossed her legs on the low leather couch while she tried to inconspicuously tug her tight, short dress down over her thighs.

Hollie, Dr. Walters's assistant, sat next to her on the designer couch, which was a relief. With Hollie's in-your face manners and Goth clothing, she didn't fit in any better than Maddy did.

Everybody was being really nice, but it was still hard not to be a bit overwhelmed by this shining silver and glass penthouse, with its fifteen-foot Christmas tree and panoramic view of downtown Seattle and Puget Sound.

Maddy had worn her only fancy dress, the one she had used to taunt Hunter before their last assignment. At least the black cocktail dress was appropriate for today's holiday festivities in James's swanky digs, which it hadn't exactly been for a meeting at the FBI office.

And Maddy felt uncomfortable with Dr. Walters and James, too. Besides their evident wealth and sophistication, they had risked their lives searching for her when they'd believed she had gone missing on the streets of Seattle. How could she ever repay them for something that momentous?

Since her parents, no one until Hunter had cared about her. But maybe Dr. Walters and James did, too, in their own way. The thought of how Maddy's fiancé loved her brought a rush of heat to her face that had nothing to do with the blazing fire.

Sitting directly across from Maddy on a matching leather couch, an observant Dr. Grayce Walters watched her closely. Maddy was trying to look sophisticated instead of like a kid in a magical toy store, but she had the feeling Dr. Walters understood every uncomfortable thought and feeling running around in her brain.

Hunter's sister Angie, James, and Mitzi, the Standard French poodle, were busy in the restaurant-sized steel kitchen, which opened to the living room with an enormous fireplace that crackled and smelled of cedar and pine. The setting was something out of a Martha Stewart magazine, complete with bouquets of red roses and holiday greens, burning bayberry candles, and Bing Crosby singing "White Christmas."

Mitzi, who belonged to Dr. Walters's boyfriend, sat in front of James, her head cocked to one side, patiently anticipating a treat. Dressed in a red shirt that matched the holiday decor and black pants, the dashing James was the host of the ladies' soiree. And from the way Angie giggled and smacked James on the shoulder, Angie had become closer to Dr. Walters's high school friend while Maddy was undercover.

Angie didn't seem at all uncomfortable with the lavish setting, but Maddy had to work not to goggle at the floor to ceiling view of Puget Sound, and the enormous Christmas tree flocked in silver, with poinsettia flowers tucked into the tree amid the silver and red balls. The tree looked like it belonged in a Nordstrom store window.

Angie emerged from the kitchen with a silver tray and crystal wineglasses. James followed with a bottle of sparkling champagne. He poured the pale liquid into each flute and added a raspberry from the bowl on Angie's tray to each glass before he passed them to his guests.

Mitzi followed the black-clad young woman walking behind James and Angie carrying a tray of unrecognizable finger foods. Hollie popped one of the red concoctions into her mouth. "I'm sure James picked the food to match his shirt."

Maddy smiled at the young woman who offered one of the gooey treats. "Goat cheese and roasted pepper."

Mitzi, who was hovering next to the young woman, pleaded at Maddy with her soulful, dark eyes.

Dr. Walters patted her lips with a red napkin. "Davis is such an easy touch. Mitzi now believes she can work her charms on everyone." Then in a soft but firm voice she said, "That's enough, Mitzi."

Mitzi trudged to Dr. Walters's chair and gave a gusty, martyred sigh when she curled up at Dr. Walter's feet.

James rolled his eyes. "Definitely a drama queen."

Hollie snickered as she raised her glass in a mock toast to James. "This from the grandest queen of all."

"You're angling for more Christmas presents?" James tilted his glass to Hollie. "We'll start the party since Aunt Aideen and Christine are coming late. They're attending a holiday luncheon for one of their charities. Which one is it today, Grayce?"

"Treehouse Services. The program that supports children in foster care."

The tops of Maddy's ear burned. Everyone in the room knew about her past as a runaway from foster care and her drug-dealing boyfriend. She didn't want these caring people to see her as a victim. She had taken control of her life when she'd joined the Marines, but it didn't mean she knew how to fit into this world of Puget Sound penthouses, French champagne, and catered parties.

Hollie leaned across the couch and touched her hand. "You know I met Dr. Walters at Teen Feed, right?" Hollie had holly leaves and berries intertwined with the twisted knot of thick, black hair at the back of her neck.

Maddy tried to mask the shock. "You volunteered there?"

Hollie laughed. Her crimson lips matched the bobbing berries. "Do I look as if I volunteered there?"

Maddy took in Hollie's 1960's black lace dress, black tie-up boots, and short red gloves.

"Dr. Walters hired me right out of the program. She and her mother volunteer there. They've given a lot of money in honor of Dr. Walters's sister. They try to help street kids."

Maddy bent down to snag a napkin from the coffee table, away from Hollie's perceptive scrutiny. Although she had been a kid on the street, she didn't want anyone to think of her as someone who couldn't take care of herself.

Hollie poked her with her elbow. "You'll get used to it."

"Used to what?"

"Being part of Dr. Walters's family. After everything we've been through together, we're bonded to you and Hunter."

Returning from the kitchen, Angie sat and scooted next to Maddy on the couch. "What's this about Hunter?"

Even with his back to the room, conferring with the caterer, James immediately turned at the mention of Hunter, his eyes wide. "Yes, do tell us how the handsome brute proposed." He walked over to a sling-back leather chair and sat down. "Come on, give Uncle Jamesie all the deets."

Embarrassment spread from her chest to her burning face. "How do you know…about our engagement?"

Angie cleared her throat. "I spilled the beans. Everyone kept asking about you and Hunter. We were all worried."

Maddy looked at everyone smiling back at her. "I really appreciate all your concern. And what you did for me when I was undercover."

Dr. Walters leaned toward Maddy. "We all appreciate the work you do, and we were glad to help."

James flicked his hand in a dramatic gesture. "Grayce loves to risk my life in these adventures. She gets bored just healing animals."

"I'm never bored with my work. And you know you love being part of the drama," Grayce said fondly.

"Drama?" Hollie snickered. "James? No way."

James crossed his legs, revealing his red-striped socks. "I want to talk weddings, since some people are stalling."

With one arched eyebrow raised, he looked directly at Dr. Walters.

"James, don't get started. It's the holiday…you know, peace and love? And don't you dare say a word about my engagement in my mother's presence."

"You need to put the poor man out of his misery."

Dr. Walters's bright green eyes danced. "Davis is in no misery."

Whatever passed between the two friends, James tossed his head and rolled his eyes. "Okay, that's a losing battle."

Dr. Walters winked at Maddy. "Tell us about your and Hunter's wedding plans."

"Nothing fancy. We're going to the courthouse with Angie and her mother. Then we'll have dinner somewhere."

"What?" James gaped. "You don't plan to invite us?"

Dr. Walters sat up. "James." Then she looked directly at Maddy. "You don't have to invite anyone you don't want to."

James continued to stare at Maddy with his dark eyes narrowed. "Of course you're going to invite all of us. We've adopted you as family, and we're not letting you pretend otherwise."

An unfamiliar feeling of belonging stirred. She shifted on the couch, not knowing where to look or what to say. She hadn't thought she had family outside of her Marine friends.

Hollie nodded at Maddy. "I told you so."

"I didn't think you'd want to…" Maddy struggled to find words but was given a reprieve by doorbell.

The caterer opened the door for Davis's Aunt Aideen and Christine, Dr. Walters's mother, and James jumped up to greet the latecomers.

Maddy was grateful for the interruption and hoped it would be the end of the wedding discussion.

Aunt Aideen's voice echoed in the high-ceilinged space. "What have we missed? Anything more about Maddy and Hunter breaking up the ISIS cell?"

"No. We just started discussing Maddy and Hunter's wedding plans," James said.

Maddy found herself sliding down on the couch. Like a Marine on a mission, James wouldn't give up until he'd achieved his objective.

Aunt Aideen, with raven-black hair and strong, angular features, was decked out in a bright red caftan with a dark green necklace and dangling earrings. Dr. Walters hugged her mom and then Aunt Aideen, who stood inches above the two petite woman.

Angie, Hollie, and Maddy all rose when the women entered the room. "Sit down, girls. No need to act like Christine and I are visiting royalty."

Hollie and Angie laughed and sat down again. Maddy followed their lead.

Christine sat next to her daughter, and Aunt Aideen sat in the other leather and steel chair. James, assisted by the caterer, handed a raspberry-garnished flute of champagne to each woman.

Aunt Aideen took a big gulp. "What are you thinking, giving me this girlie drink? Where's my Scotch?"

"Well, you're ruining one of my Christmas surprises." He pointed to a brightly foil-wrapped package under the Christmas tree.

"Do I have to wait the two weeks until Christmas day to drink my Scotch?"

"No, of course not."

James nodded to the caterer standing behind the well-polished kitchen island. She immediately brought out a glass filled with a rich, amber-colored liquid. James had anticipated and prepared for Aunt Aideen's insistence on Scotch.

James sat back down in the chair and crossed his legs. "Maddy just announced that she and Hunter are going to be married at the courthouse."

Maddy wanted to disappear between the couch cushions.

Aunt Aideen pointed her finger at Maddy. "Your marriage must be celebrated at my home. And my friend, Judge Jefferson, can marry you if you don't have a military person available to do the service."

Maddy had thought about asking Colonel Dawson, but it was the holidays and she couldn't ask him to fly up for the ceremony.

Aunt Aideen focused her steely gaze on Maddy. "I have a giant house with plenty of room for all the guests."

Aunt Aideen's commanding presence and forceful will reminded her of her sergeant in basic training. Not someone to ignore. "But, ma'am, we don't have any guests."

Aunt Aideen guffawed. "I predict a real crowd."

Angie had told Maddy that Aunt Aideen considered herself a psychic and read Tarot cards.

"You have all of us." Aunt Aideen gestured with her long arm. "And then Hunter will want to invite his friends as well."

Maddy felt like a ship off its mooring. She took a big swig of champagne. Hunter never said whether he'd like to invite his friends, only that he wanted to marry her.

Angie, the traitor, added, "It would be great to include our group from the VA hospital."

And Maddy had wanted to include her PTSD group. They had formed a deep bond that was hard to explain to people who hadn't served.

Dr. Walters leaned forward on the couch. "Maddy, don't let them railroad you into anything you don't want. They're good at that."

"So says the woman who is keeping everyone in nuptial limbo," James said.

Dr. Walters closed her eyes and took a deep breath. Her mother patted her hand.

"Grayce and Davis will decide when the time is right," Christine said.

James shook his head. "I've been waiting for years to plan her wedding."

"But now you can take over Maddy and Hunter's," Angie chimed in. "My brother and Maddy are Marines. They don't know the first thing about planning weddings."

Maddy was surprised by Angie's response. Since she had never discussed her childhood with anyone, Angie had no way of knowing Maddy had always dreamed about her wedding. Just because she was a Marine didn't mean she was different from any other red-blooded female. Did any girl ever forget her dreams of a perfect wedding?

"Hunter and I were planning to get married in Seattle so Angie can be with us. We have to report back to San Diego for reassignment after the New Year. Besides, no one can plan a wedding in two weeks."

James puffed up. "Oh, ye of little faith. Listen, honey, I can do a wedding in two days if need be. And two weeks is hardly a challenge. But with the holiday..." His eyes shone with anticipation.

Aunt Aideen sat back in her chair. "Tut, tut. James will do the flowers and the wedding clothes. I've got a great caterer. Marcello can do anything. What kind of food would you like?"

Maddy couldn't decide whether she needed to cry, hug someone, or escape the overwhelming feelings swamping her because everyone was treating her like family. "I'll need to talk with Hunter."

"Hunter doesn't strike me as the type to care about wedding planning...more like wedding nights. What a tasty...with all that muscle and menace." James shook his head. "You and Grayce definitely like the dark, brooding types."

Flashing on last night with an insatiable Hunter, her face flushed, and she mutely nodded at James. Aware of her champagne buzz and the instability of her high heels, Maddy stood carefully and headed to the bathroom. She needed a little breathing space, away from everyone's close and interested inspection.

In the bathroom, Maddy splashed cold water on her bright cheeks, trying to cool her face and her agitated feelings. Everything in her life had changed in the last weeks. Her life had taken too many turns too quickly—first Hunter's devotion, and now a group of caring friends. It took some getting used to for a woman who had been alone. She had no idea how to react to suddenly being surrounded by love and care.

When she exited the shiny, black bathroom with its fragrant candles and matching towels, Dr. Walters and Mitzi awaited her in the hall.

From her study of martial arts, Maddy was able to focus for calm, deadly force. Dr. Walters channeled her energy into an aura that surrounded her with calming reassurance.

Dr. Walters gently touched her arm. "Maddy, this is your wedding. You can have it any way you want. James means well, but you get who he is…"

What could Maddy say? James was Dr. Walters's best friend. She had only met him once after Dr. Walters's kidnapping.

"I like James. He's interesting."

"Everyone has the same response on meeting James. He always has his own vision." Dr. Walters laughed, a laugh that was gentle and exuded kindness. "I sensed you need a break away from the group and their plans for your wedding. How about we go into James's study for a few minutes?"

Maddy let out a breath she had been holding since preparing herself to face everyone again. "That would be great."

Dr. Walters opened the door next to bathroom. Obviously comfortable here, Mitzi dashed in. The living room was edgy in black and metal; this room was sunny and warm, with lemony yellow walls. "This is James's man cave."

There was a large TV on one wall, and two soft leather loungers in a light, buttery color. Bright-colored art of all shapes and forms covered another wall. No sports posters on any wall for James's man cave.

Dr. Walters spun one lounger toward Maddy and sat on the other. Mitzi approached and put her head on Maddy's lap. Maddy didn't have a lot of experience with dogs, but she ran her hand along the poodle's head. Mitzi closed her eyes, content to be petted.

"Don't feel obliged to pat Mitzi. She knows a softie when she sees one."

Why did Maddy feel as if Dr. Walters wasn't only talking about Mitzi?

"What do you really want for your wedding, Maddy?"

"Honestly, I haven't had much time to think. Everything has happened so fast with our reassignment. We want to get married as quickly as possible to not be separated."

"Then a fast wedding makes sense." Dr. Walters smiled at Maddy. "Angie said you're a Marine and not interested in weddings."

Maddy smiled back. "I wasn't always a Marine. I was like all girls—dolls, coloring, dress-up. My mother painted my toenails and fingernails. And my dad called me his 'little princess.'"

"Your parents sound wonderful. I'm sure they would be proud of the man you've chosen. Of course I might be a little biased since Hunter rescued me from the kidnappers."

Maddy nodded. "My parents would have loved Hunter."

"Have you thought about what your parents would have wanted for your wedding?"

Maddy swallowed down the powerful emotions stuck in her throat. She had never shared any memories of her parents before. They had been all tucked inside her heart, never to be opened so they wouldn't come tumbling out and crush her with grief. "I hadn't really thought it through. It's been so sudden."

"I lost my sister when I was about the same age as when you lost your parents. My sister, Cassie, was my best friend and confidante. You remind me of her. All energetic and ready for a dare."

"Hollie did tell me that you and your mother volunteer in honor of your sister. So generous of you."

"Volunteering helps soften our loss. It's healing for both of us. So would sharing your wedding."

"But, but..." Her heart thumped against her chest while her stomach rolled. She shifted in the comfortable chair.

"I understand about rushing through the wedding and not making a big deal about it because you won't have to dwell doing it without having your parents there."

Maddy shook her head. She wasn't avoiding anything. There was no need to stir up old feelings. She just wanted to marry Hunter.

"I see the similarities in our situations. It's hard to trust the future after your whole world falls apart."

Mitzi stood and curled her body along Dr. Walters's feet. The dog was amazing, reading all the emotions spinning through the room.

"I've been hesitant about making wedding plans myself and could not for the life of me understand why, since Davis is an incredible man. But I just realized in the past couple of weeks that the wedding will stir up all the old grief. I didn't want to put my parents, or maybe myself, through the pain of my sister's absence."

Maddy fought the sting of tears. "It's hard to remember what my life was like before..."

Dr. Walters spoke quietly. "You've had no one to share your past. My parents and I have each other to remember all the good times. Can you let us share your wedding with you? I'm sure your parents would love to see you with people who care about you."

Maddy felt the awful burn behind her eyes as the tears streaked down her cheeks. She never cried. The idea of her parents happy for her triggered way too many feelings for even a tough Marine.

She choked on a half-sob, half-laugh. "I always did want to look like a fairy princess, with a white gown that swirled."

Dr. Walters reached across the space between the chairs and took Maddy's hand. "Will you let us be part of your wedding? Sharing in the joy of your very special moment?"

Maddy nodded. And, just like that, Maddy had a wedding to share. Everything her girlish heart had always hoped for.

CHAPTER TWO

Hunter took a swig of the holiday microbrew, fortifying himself before Drew arrived at the Tippe and Drague Alehouse. He was about to spring a shock, an earthquake-caliber shock, on his marriage-phobic Special Forces buddy—that he would be getting married in ten days, with all the bells and whistles.

The event had grown into Maddy's dream wedding. The venue would be Aunt Aideen's house, with the Colonel flying in to perform the ceremony. Hunter didn't care one bit about the ceremony or who would be there, as long as Maddy was happy and he finally had her as his wife. He was glad Dr. Walters and her friends had adopted Maddy, and the women and James were going over the top with the wedding details. Maddy deserved every bit of their attention and love.

Hunter hadn't planned to invite his friends, but Maddy had insisted. And there was the problem. Drew, his best friend, would demand an explanation of why Hunter had drastically reversed his views on women and marriage. How could he explain love to someone who was more cynical and jaded than he had been? He and Drew had sworn together that they'd never buy into the illusion of happily ever after.

They had never discussed the origins of their aversion to marriage. Hunter always knew his mother's desertion had played a big part in his refusal to commit to one woman. He knew nothing about Drew's past except that his parents were divorced and he had been engaged at one point.

Hunter scanned the small pub—mostly men and women in flannel shirts, boots, and North Face jackets. Seattle was unseasonably cold for December, usually a month of darkness and rain. Because of the crisp, cold weather, Maddy was hoping it would snow on their wedding day. With her bright baby-blues lit up in wonder, she got breathless envisioning the magic of a snowy, Christmas Eve wedding. If he had any control over the weather, he'd make the white magic appear for Maddy.

His Marine buddies had ribbed him when he called to invite them to the wedding. But if they had any idea the lengths their tough-ass buddy would go to make Maddy happy, he'd never hear the end of the digs about leg shackles, marriage traps, and being pussy-whipped.

But Drew wouldn't be into the usual male razzing. He would want the truth. He and Drew had thrived on being the lone wolves—not needing anyone, not relying on anyone. Of course, specializing in intelligence work did make you leery about trusting people. How could Hunter admit now that everything he'd said, before Maddy, about women and love was ignorant and self-protecting?

Hunter wasn't much of a drinker, but he took another gulp when he spotted Drew walk into the Beacon Hill watering hole.

Drew saw Hunter immediately and quickly made his way through the wall-to-wall crowd using his imposing size and presence. He bent over the wood table and shook Hunter's hand. "Hey, man."

Hunter stood. He didn't have to look up to many men, but Drew, six-foot five and built like a linebacker, was one of the few.

"What brings you to town?" Drew pulled out the wooden chair and sat down across from Hunter.

"My sister."

"You never said your sister lived in Seattle."

Hunter shrugged. "Why would I? You're not from here."

"I'm going to be here now. I just got transferred."

Drew had become more secretive about his assignments when he transferred out of military intelligence. Hunter expected he was now NSA or CIA.

"FBI?" Hunter always asked, knowing it was futile, but that didn't stop him from prodding.

Drew's smile was slow and easy. "Yeah, something like that."

Hunter glanced at Drew's black thermal shirt and worn jeans. "You don't look like Feeb."

"What the hell? You the fashion police now?"

Hunter laughed. "Nah, just glad you're in town since I've got a favor to ask."

"You want me to set you up for New Year's?" Drew's success in attracting women made Hunter look like a monk.

Hunter, thinking of Maddy's reaction to Drew's proposal, couldn't suppress a bark of laughter. "I'm already set."

"Well, aren't you the man!"

Hunter waved over the waitress, who was dressed all in black—high, black boots and a tight, black T-shirt tucked into her jeans. The twenty-something woman did a slow perusal of Drew's outstretched muscular legs.

Drew gave the woman his best predatory smile. "I'll have what he's drinking, honey."

The woman fluttered her heavily made-up eyelashes and smiled coyly. "Sure thing, honey."

Hunter watched Drew's eyes follow the waitress's slow, hip-swinging saunter. It was just like old times, with Drew on the make. "Looks like you're not having any trouble adjusting to being back in Seattle."

Drew lifted his arms over his head and shifted his hefty size in the small chair. "How long are you in town?"

"I'm here until after the New Year."

"Two stewardesses from my flight back have a layover in Seattle on New Year's Eve. If you want to ditch your plans, we can party with them. It'll be like old times."

"Flight back from where?"

Drew's brow furrowed. "You don't trust my judgement? Remember our layover in Budapest?"

While the waitress set the beers on the table, Drew got the familiar gleam in his green eyes that signaled he was about to recount one of their sexual escapades that Hunter would rather forget. He felt like he would be betraying Maddy by reminiscing about his single-man's exploits.

"Forget the women. The favor I need is something you're not going to like."

"Shit. You want me to take your sister out on New Year's Eve."

"My sister?" Hunter barked. "That's hilarious. My sister is not the kind of woman who'd be interested in someone like you."

"What the hell does that mean? Sisters always like me."

"Sorry, man. Nothing about you, but my sister doesn't get around."

"What? She look like your old man?"

Hunter leaned across the table, invading Drew's space. "My sister is fine. She just isn't a player. She's had a rough time since her last assignment in Afghanistan and definitely doesn't need a sexual cowboy."

"Take a breath, dude. When did you become the protective big brother?

"Since I'm marrying her best friend."

Drew froze with his glass in midair. Hunter fought the impulse to laugh out loud at the bewildered look on the face of his fellow covert officer, who had been thoroughly trained not to show emotion.

Then Drew started choking, coughing in spasms, his fair skin mottled a deep red. "What the hell? You trying to kill me? You're not getting married. You don't believe in marriage any more than I do."

"I'm getting married on Christmas Eve."

"Is this some kind of joke? You never said a word when I talked to you last month."

"I couldn't talk about it because Maddy and I were undercover."

Drew ran his fingers through his sandy brown hair, causing clumps to stand up in irregular spikes. "Are you crazy? You know you can't trust feelings when you're undercover."

Hunter was glad Maddy couldn't hear this. Otherwise, she would have gotten the wrong impression of his closest friend.

"You had sex during your assignment, and now you feel like you have to marry her? You always were an honorable son-of-a-bitch."

Hunter shook his head. "It's not like that at all. When you meet Maddy, you'll understand."

Drew raised his eyebrows.

"Okay, you won't understand. But Maddy's the right woman for me. You can't understand because you haven't met the right woman."

"I can't believe this. The most cynical man I know spouting bullshit about the right woman? Look, I get it. You got hot and heavy undercover, but it isn't real. It's lust, man."

Hunter wasn't the kind of man who wanted to explain his feelings, but he felt his friend deserved an explanation. He and Drew had been in many tight spots together, and he trusted the man with his life. "It isn't just lust. Maddy helps my life make sense. And all I can think about is making her happy. Lust is definitely part of it, but it's more than the sex."

"You must have been tortured on your last assignment, or you've been reprogrammed, or had a chip inserted in your brain. Hunter Hines would never say sex isn't the big draw. I know…"

Hunter shook his head. He had tried. "You don't have to buy into the whole marriage thing, but I'd really like you to be there for me. Will you be my best man?"

Drew narrowed his eyes, then gave the boyish grin that melted women's hearts. "Of course. You know I'll be there for you. And I'll keep my reservations to myself since I wouldn't want to offend the little lady."

"Oh, I don't think you have to worry about offending Maddy. She can hold her own."

CHAPTER THREE

Maddy stood in front of the mirror and tried to strike a nonchalant pose. She refused to be intimidated by a ritzy dress designer when she wasn't frightened by battle-tough Marines. Maddy doubted many Marines had ever come to this fancy, schmantzy Fourth Avenue dress store. Probably Bill Gates's wife bought her dresses right here from Julie Lang, but not the likes of Maddy, who was outfitted in her usual black turtleneck sweater, black slacks, and leather boots.

Julie, in a slim, charcoal-gray skirt, a white blouse and sling-back heels, and her thick, black hair pulled back in a ponytail, didn't match what Maddy had envisioned for an exclusive dress designer. But her understated, youthful appearance fit the style of the shop to a T. Although the store sparkled with white gowns, tiaras, and rows of stylish high heels, everything had a graceful simplicity and sophistication, much like its owner.

The usually irreverent James couldn't contain his enthusiasm. His dark eyes gleamed at the elegant surroundings and the fashion discussion. "Thank you for fitting us into your calendar on such short notice. I would have hated to go to Naomi B."

"Your timing is perfect. I've just finished all the gowns for the Debutante Ball," Julie said.

A champagne glass in hand, James paced around the stylish space filled with French furniture, crystal chandeliers, and opulent mirrors. "As we discussed on the phone, we need

Maddy's wedding gown quickly. I'm thinking something in an off-white, perhaps pale pink."

Julie stood next to James and studied Maddy. "With her color, more of a warm white or ivory, no blues or gray in the white."

Maddy was definitely out of her league. She had no idea that the color white required so much consideration.

James smiled at Maddy. "My vision is that Maddy should look like a snow maiden out of a fairytale. And the dress must swirl."

A snow maiden sounded perfect to Maddy. She had shared only with Hunter that she hoped there would be snow on Christmas Eve for her wedding.

James referred to what she had shared about "swirling" with Dr. Walters. Maddy might have been offended, but Dr. Walters had treated her almost-mocking comment with total seriousness. And the sympathetic woman had understood better than Maddy how much she wanted to feel like a princess—in a dress that swirled.

"And for the maid of honor dress, a deep red—not any orange tones for Angie with her olive skin. I'm doing all white flowers—hydrangeas, orchids, roses. I want Angie to be the holiday color."

Angie, seated in a blue velvet chair, sipped champagne and didn't say a word. Maddy stuck to drinking water, since she wanted to remember every moment of this day and the design of her dream wedding gown. She didn't imagine she'd be coming back for more gowns in the future. Designer gowns were definitely not in her pay grade.

She and Hunter had agreed that it would offend Dr. Walters and her mother to try to reimburse them for their gift. Instead, they'd decided they would make a donation to Teen Feed in honor of Dr. Walters's sister, Cassie. They also hadn't told Angie, but they planned to pay for her dress.

Julie, standing next to James, carefully studied both women.

It was difficult not to flinch under her close inspection.

"Angie, what do you think?" Maddy asked.

"I'm fashion challenged so I have no idea, but I think you looking like a fairy queen is perfect."

Maddy tried to imagine Hunter's response to seeing her in in a flowing white wedding gown. He repeatedly reassured her that she was beautiful to him no matter what she wore.

"What do you want to wear, Angie?"

"You're the bride. What I'm wearing is not important."

"But are you okay with wearing red? Because you can pick any color you want."

"James already informed me that red is my color. He wants me in red high heels to show off my fabulous legs. How can I argue with the man? I've always wanted red high heels. And I've never had a red dress, so this will be fun."

James ran his hand over his impeccably styled hair as he spoke to Julie. "My only indecision is what to do with Maddy's hair and whether to do a veil or hat. Of course, it will depend on the dress."

"Only one indecision?" Julie's lips curved slightly. Maddy wasn't sure if she was teasing. "Neither. Her stunning blue eyes should be the focal point. Besides, Maddy doesn't strike me as a veil person." If Maddy hadn't been trained in reading people's body language, she would have missed the way the designer's shoulders straightened as her tone got more precise. Julie didn't force her opinions. She was too skilled to offend her clients, but, like James, she also had definite views.

"I have the perfect dress for Maddy. I had planned to put the gown in the window for my holiday window display."

Maddy had been stunned by the beautiful window display. It was like something out of *Vogue*, the white gowns in the window glistening and glimmering like the backdrop of snow and silver lights.

"Julie's window is my favorite in the entire downtown area. It's also a prime marketing space," James added.

Maddy's heart thundered in anticipation.

Julie walked toward the back of the shop. Her assistant, who had been hovering in the background, followed Julie into the back room.

James raised his dark eyebrows. "Julie loves lace and silks, but I'm thinking more organza for the skirt to make it the best for twirling and swirling."

Maddy held her breath. She didn't know squat about the difference between silks and organza.

Angie squeezed her hand. "I can't believe you're going to be a bride. And to my brother. Life has the craziest twists."

"Nothing is going to change our friendship. You know that, right?"

"I know. Now you are officially my sister."

Maddy squeezed Angie's hand back. "You've always been my family, but now I get both you and Hunter."

James coughed dramatically. "Did I hear the mention of family?"

Maddy had been waiting for the perfect moment. She stepped toward James. "You and Dr. Walters are family, too. Hunter and I will never be able to repay you for the kindness."

"Nothing to repay. I love weddings." He paused. "Well, you could introduce me to one of Hunter's friends."

Maddy grabbed James's arm. "I can do that. But I have one more favor to ask."

James dragged out the words. "One more?"

"Since Aunt Aideen plans to have an aisle in her living room, would you be willing to give me away?"

The shock on James's face was priceless. It had never occurred to Maddy that she might surprise the sophisticated man. He took out a pristine handkerchief and patted his tearing eyes. His voice was strained, and he swallowed with effort. "I'd be honored to give you away, but you know we're never *giving you away*." And then he pulled Maddy into his arms and hugged her tightly.

After she had ran from her foster family eight years ago, she had believed she would never find the feeling of family again. But her wandering had brought her around to the truth. Family was made from the heart. And though her parents were gone, she was building a new family.

The wedding would be perfect, not because of the perfect dress or flowers, but because of the love that surrounded her.

And at that precise moment, Julie carried out the perfect dress for Maddy. A frothy cloud of ivory lace and silk.

James beamed at Julie and then turned to Maddy. "What do you think?"

"It's beautiful."

And now it was her turn to cry. She rubbed her eyes, trying to hide her tears. Marines didn't cry.

"The simple lace sweetheart bodice will enhance your curves, but the textured, layered organza of the skirt is perfect for swirling." And then the quiet, understated woman's mouth curved into a smile that reached to her eyes. Julie must have a need to be a fairy godmother, since her fanciful designs created princesses.

"The neckline will work wonderfully with the pearl necklace and drop earrings that Aunt Aideen is lending Maddy for 'something borrowed,'" James added.

Maddy touched the fabric reverently. She had never imagined anything more beautiful or wonderful.

"Maddy shouldn't wear anything in her hair. Pearls will be the perfect complement to the dress. The sheen of the pearls against her dewy skin will balance the whimsy of the skirt," Julie said.

Angie moved next to Maddy. "You're going to look beautiful. And I can't wait to see Hunter's face when he sees you in this dress. The tough woman who can decimate an enemy—all girly."

James looked at Angie. "Maddy isn't going to be the only one who will look gorgeous. A short, red sheath hugging your drop-dead body? You'll be devastating, Angie! But, Julie, I'm not sure about Angie's hair. What do you think up or down?"

Maddy was surprised at how often James, brimming with self-confidence, deferred to Julie.

Maddy was glad that he and Julie were both brilliant in design and fashion since she had no skill in that area. She gave the same kind of focus to her training and missions. When it came to things like which flowers would wilt or which whites looked good in candlelight, she deferred to the experts.

Julie stepped back and stared at Angie as if she were a painting in the art museum. "Her hair should be pulled back in a chignon to showcase her cheekbones. I have the perfect dangling earrings for her. With her natural beauty and height, I'd like her to have straight but elegant lines as a contrast to Maddy's soft, romantic look."

Angie's face was turning a bright shade of red. "The wedding isn't about me. It's Maddy's day."

James put his arm around Angie. They were almost the same height. "Maddy is the bride, but there isn't any reason for you not to have girlfriend fun. Besides, Hunter told me he has invited a lot of his Marine buddies. Which is why you and I both have to look scrumptious."

Angie snickered. "I've had enough of Marines. They're all yours, James."

"You've had your fill of Marines? Interesting!"

Angie punched James in the arm.

James rubbed the spot. "That hurt."

Angie laughed. "No whining from you. I know you work out every day."

"Margot, take Maddy into the fitting room while I help Angie and James."

Maddy followed the tall blonde, who was also wearing the simple but elegant Julie look. The day couldn't get any better.

CHAPTER FOUR

Hunter, the Colonel, and Drew stood in Aunt Aideen's library waiting to be called for the ceremony. Through the pane-glass windows he could see could see falling snow beginning to blanket the Queen Anne neighborhood. Maddy must be ecstatic that her wish for a snowy Christmas Eve wedding had come true.

"Sir, it means a great deal to Maddy and me that you were willing to come on Christmas Eve to perform this service," Hunter said.

"I've got a special spot for Maddy. She is the daughter we never had. My wife would've loved to have had a daughter. Three sons, three Marines."

"I hope you won't have any trouble getting to the airport, sir."

"I'm sorry I can't stay for the celebration. But I know how Seattle closes down when it snows."

Hunter tried to keep the conversation going with the Colonel, but all he could think about was Maddy. Was she excited, nervous? He had so much wanted to share Maddy's day. She told him about her conversation with Dr. Walters, and how she had realized how much she would miss her parents on her wedding day.

He didn't want her to feel alone. It had been only twenty-four hours since he kissed her goodnight before she spent her last night as a single woman with Angie. After today, he would never spend another night without her.

He could hear Aunt Aideen's commanding voice directing the guests to their seats in the living room. James had decorated the entire house with flowers. The chairs lining the living room had white ribbons and bouquets attached to each aisle seat. White candles burned throughout the house, and the flowery fragrances blended with the smell of pine from the giant Christmas tree standing in the front window.

Two bars were set up on each side of the library, where the twenty-five guests would gather after the ceremony. While the guests had drinks and appetizers, the staff would remove the chairs from the living room and set up tables for dinner. Everything had been orchestrated as flawlessly as a well-organized military operation by James and Aunt Aideen.

Hunter checked his watch again. He didn't want to admit it, but he had the same nervous tension building in his body that he experienced before a dangerous operation, in spite of the fact that this wasn't an assignment and there was no threat. This was the beginning of his mission to protect and care for Maddy for the rest of his life.

James entered the library in a black tuxedo with a white rose on his lapel. The debonair man looked like he had just stepped out of a James Bond movie. "You're one lucky man. Maddy is more gorgeous than I'd anticipated. Maddy and Angie are both spectacular women, so I have to admit they made my job easy."

Hunter had started to resent James and all the time Maddy had spent planning the wedding with him. But seeing how happy she was, he couldn't really be upset. And it was obvious that James cared for Maddy.

"Is Maddy okay?"

"She's more than okay. She is radiant and excited and pleased as can be that it snowed."

It didn't sound like Maddy was having bridal jitters. He might be more nervous than his bride.

"Colonel, I've arranged for a car service to take you to the airport," James said.

"Thank you. I'm sorry I can't stay, but I can't miss Christmas Eve with my grandkids."

James stiffened and looked at Drew. "May I have a private word with you?"

Drew, in his Special Forces formal dress uniform, was leaning against the wall next to the window. Hunter and the Colonel wore their Marine dress uniforms, as did all his buddies. The only Marines not in uniform were Maddy and Angie.

Drew laughed. "No need. I truly can handle the ring business."

James's dark eyes narrowed. "I'm not worried about the ring. It will only take a minute."

Drew shrugged his shoulders. "Sure."

James gave a slight bow of his head. "Gentleman, excuse us." He looked at his watch. "Only seven minutes before you take your places."

James walked away with Drew following.

Colonel looked at Hunter. "Drew's in trouble again. And why do I think it's about a woman?"

Hunter watched the two men standing outside the door talking. James was definitely incensed about something. His face was red, and he was poking his finger into Drew's chest. Whatever had James hot under the collar, he didn't care about the consequences of provoking Drew—or he had a death wish.

If Drew had offended one of Maddy's friends last night at the rehearsal dinner, Hunter was going to kick his ass—after the wedding, of course. Except Drew was a smooth player and wouldn't push any boundaries that a woman didn't want pushed.

The ultimate alpha, Drew—who outweighed James by fifty pounds—stepped back and nodded. The Colonel winked at Hunter, amused by Drew's submissive response.

James looked again at his watch, then stepped back into the library. "Are you ready to take your places? Colonel, you will go out first. Is there anything you need?"

"Nothing. If you or Aunt Aideen want to join the Marines, I'm always in need of good sergeants."

James rubbed his chin, pretending to contemplate the possibility. "I would get so tired of wearing the same uniform over and over again." And then the ballsy man winked at the Colonel.

The Colonel responded with a loud guffaw.

James looked directly at Hunter. "Give the Colonel and Aunt Aideen a few minutes, and then come out." Hunter felt his heart kick against his chest. He was finally going to make Maddy his wife.

The Colonel slapped him on the back. "Never seen that look before, Hunter. Pure terror from the man who was willing to take on the Taliban singlehandedly." The Colonel rubbed his hands together. "This a great day for my little Maddy. Never officiated a wedding where both the bride and groom were Marines."

Aunt Aideen, in a billowing emerald green dress, marched into the room. "It's our time, Colonel. Let me escort you to your spot."

The Colonel offered Aunt Aideen his arm. "Let me escort you, my lady."

Aunt Aideen fanned her face. "I always did have a soft spot for a man in uniform."

Drew waited at the doorway while the Colonel and Aunt Aideen exited. He looked at Hunter. "Are you ready?"

Hunter shook his head. "We're supposed to give them a few minutes. Just enough time for you to explain what that little side conversation with James was about."

"Nothing to concern you on your wedding day," Drew said laconically.

"What did you do to get James riled up?"

"I think the wedding planning has gotten to his nerves."

Hunter grabbed his arm. "Spill it."

"It really isn't anything. Your sister didn't like me joking with some of the guys about getting hitched."

"That's it?"

"She got all fiery about defending you."

"That doesn't sound like Angie. She's really easygoing."

Drew stopped. "No she's not. She's…"

Hunter would have to finish this conversation later. He needn't worry about his sister, she could take care of herself. Besides, it was time to marry Maddy.

"Let's go." Hunter's heart raced, and his palms were sweaty. He looked straight ahead as he took his spot next to the Colonel in the packed living room. Drew followed and positioned himself next to Hunter.

Everything happened in a blur. The Colonel nodding to him, Angie coming down the aisle, stunning all in red. Hunter didn't really know much about music, but Angie moved gracefully with the music despite her impressively high heels.

And instead of turning to her place, she walked straight to Hunter and hugged him tightly. She whispered, "I'm so glad you came to Seattle." Tears were in her eyes as she stared into his. Eyes that looked just like his and his father's.

If he hadn't come to find his missing sister, he'd never have met Maddy. He hugged Angie so tight that he felt her breath tighten. "Me, too."

Angie stepped into her spot across from him. And they all waited until the church music changed to "Love is All Around." Everyone in the room stood and faced the foyer.

And then Maddy emerged. She was magnificent in a white fluffy gown, her blond curls bobbing. From across the room, he could see her blue eyes focused on him. His heart swelled with possessiveness and love.

James held her arm as they started toward him. The song matched the feeling in the room. Love was all around because of Maddy. She was love incarnate. Her eyes sparkled like the snowy night. She took her time coming down the aisle, smiling first at her VA group, then at Dr. Walters and her parents, and finally at Aunt Aideen. He understood. Everyone was under her spell. He hadn't been to many weddings and didn't know how brides were supposed to act, but Maddy's genuine joy enveloped everyone.

James had tears in his eyes when he presented her to Hunter. He felt a primitive satisfaction when James placed Maddy's hand onto Hunter's. "Take good care of my princess." James's voice broke. He turned and sat next to Aunt Aideen in the front row, dabbing at his eyes with a red handkerchief.

Hunter took Maddy's arm, pulling her next to his side. She never took her eyes away from his face. James was right. Maddy didn't look like the tough Marine. She was a snow angel or a princess, a feminine love goddess, and now she belonged to him.

He didn't care that he was supposed to wait to say it. He didn't care what anyone thought. "I love you, Maddy, now and forever."

Maddy's blue eyes softened. "Now and forever, Hunter."

EPILOGUE

Drew took his spot next to Hunter in the lavish living room. Trained in subterfuge, he gave no indication that he was he was steaming mad—in fact, seething. Not his usual MO, but since he excelled in clandestine work, he could easily pretend that he was happy to see his friend tie the death knot. He could overlook that his friend had moved on without him and pretend that he didn't want to take down the suave jerk who had the nerve to reprimand him like he was some sort of primitive Neanderthal.

So what. He had made a joke with the other guys. Guys made crude comments all the time. It was just bad timing that Hunter's sister had heard him say Maddy had cut off Hunter's balls. Shit, Angie was a Marine. She had heard worse. Hunter wouldn't care. He had made the same jokes about marriage for years.

Drew would apologize and just hoped he hadn't said aloud that she was as fierce as an Amazon when she was so incensed.

Putting on his most convincing smile, he turned toward the foyer in unison with Hunter. "From This Moment On" by Shania Twain was playing. And Angie, dressed in a knock 'em dead red dress and high heels showcasing her long, shapely legs, stepped into the living room.

The sight of the incredible woman was like a sucker-punch to his chest, leaving him staggering from the impact. The bouquet of red roses she held in her hands shook slightly. Her friends must have said something to her, because she laughed—a husky sound that carried throughout the spacious room. Her face softened, and she started to walk toward him.

And for some unfathomable, primitive reason, he was glad she was walking toward him. Drew glanced over at Hunter's Marine buddies. They were definitely having the same male response hammering through their bodies at the sight of this sexy, beautiful woman.

Angie stopped and petted the Army dog sitting next to Hollie and her boyfriend. Drew would never have believed that dogs would be allowed at such a fancy wedding, but the Army dog wasn't the only one. Dr. Walters's poodle had been sitting next to her in the second row.

Hollie, the Goth, must have made a joke when Angie was bent over. Angie rolled her eyes and laughed again—a low, throaty sound that made his manly parts take notice. And he found himself, like everyone else in the room, smiling with her.

Drew took the two steps toward her, his heartbeat ratcheting up. And a startling possessiveness shot through him, a deep need to claim her.

She barely glanced at him. And instead of taking his arm so he could escort her, she walked to her brother. She wrapped her arms around Hunter and whispered. Drew first saw surprise on Hunter's face and then a tender look as he squeezed her tight.

Angie then stepped to her spot, and he could see the tears pooling in her dark eyes. She glanced up at him, her eyes still open with love before she looked away. And some small part of the cold chill in his heart melted.

During the ceremony, he kept stealing glances at Angie, but she never once looked at him. She cried when Hunter kissed Maddy at the end of the ceremony. And she and Maddy embraced before the newlywed couple went down the aisle while friends pelted them with flower petals.

She watched wistfully while Maddy and Hunter paused along their way to greet their guests, and an unfamiliar urge to protect stirred within him. He wanted to take away her pensive look, to protect her from any pain. He never wanted her to be alone or to suffer. He didn't want to think about what had happened to her in Afghanistan.

He tried to catch her eye when he offered his arm to escort her down the aisle. She kept her gaze averted. He whispered to her, "Smile, it's a happy occasion."

Her eyes were dewy and beautiful with unshed tears when she looked up at him. And he had the most insane need to kiss her. And she gave that same deep, husky laugh that caused electrical currents to race up his spine. "I thought you believed there was a lot of pain involved with weddings."

Unable to speak, he stared at her sparkling, dark eyes, her red full lips, and the little dimple that formed on her right check when she smiled.

"Speechless," she said, eyebrows arched. "Now that's something new for the mighty soldier." And, with a challenging smirk, she took his arm. "It must be because you're almost finished with your painful duties."

And at that precise moment, he changed his mind about the pain associated with weddings.

Enjoy an excerpt from

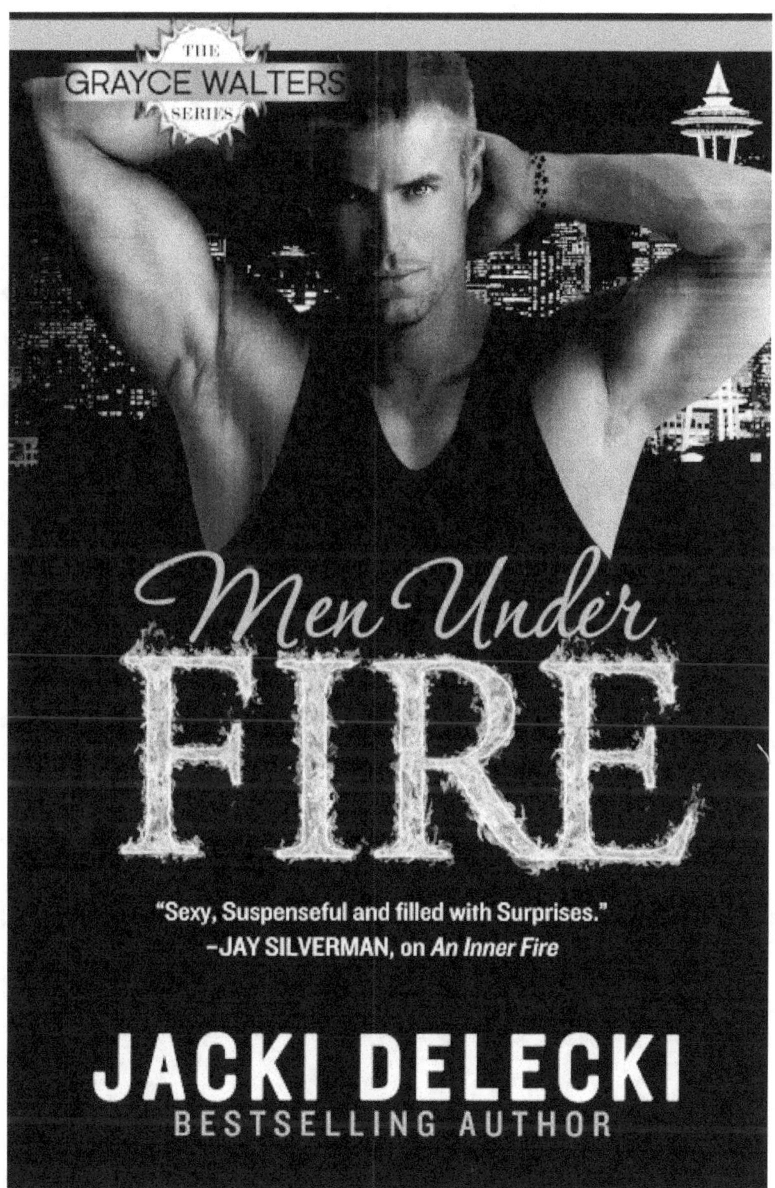

EXCERPT

Hollie Thomas headed down Thirty-Fourth to the copy place with Sgt. Welby and his dog. Hollie's long strides couldn't match Sgt. Welby's. She almost had to run to keep up. He was quiet and tense as they dodged people on the sidewalk. Talley also appeared to be on duty, her entire body alert with her head held high.

Hollie peeked from underneath her eyelashes to look up at the impressive soldier. The sunlight glistened on his angular face and forehead. He definitely had the whole stud package going for him—tall, broad shoulders, sandy-blond hair, and killer bright eyes. He was unlike any man she had known. Like the heroes in the movies, he had the penetrating blue eyes of Ryan Gosling and the boy-next-door look of Chris Hemsworth. Although not as big as the Marvel comic book hero Thor, Sgt. Welby looked as if he could hammer anyone who got in his way.

He looked down at her right as she was checking him out.

Oh, shit.

His full lips curved into a full-wattage, sexy smile. Did he know what his smile did to women? She guessed that he knew the impact of his boyish face and crinkly blue eyes. He must have women throwing themselves at him all the time.

"A penny for your thoughts?"

Oh, buggers. "I was wondering what the tat is on your wrist. Battles you've fought?"

His lashes shuttered down as his jaw muscles tightened. "They're in honor of men from my unit who died."

Going from bad to worse. "I'm sorry."

"It's fine. Lots of people ask," he answered in an abrupt voice she hadn't heard before. His azure eyes stared back at her, and his lip curled into a quirky smile. "I like your tat."

Man, he was adept at switching things up. She wasn't bad at banter, but with Sgt. Welby, the game felt different, exhilarating. She gave him back her best radioactive smile and asked in a sultry voice, "Which one?" Let his mind spin on that for a while. She had never tried to mess with the Captain America types, but she knew how to deal with the assholes on the street.

He stopped mid-step. A little joy buoyed up inside her. She liked getting a reaction from him. She had spent the entire time when he'd come into the office ignoring his hot, forceful stares and trying to hide her reaction.

He gave out a long whistle between his teeth. Good to know she could get to him. "You know you're playing a dangerous game."

She widened her eyes, feigning total innocence. "I've no idea what you're talking about."

He pulled back, his squared chin tucked in, and looked at her from her sandals up her legs to her chest before looking at her face.

Captured like a deer in the headlights by Nick's intensity, she didn't squirm and, she hoped to God, didn't reveal how nervous he made her with his piercing stare. She felt the heat and the scrutiny as if he were touching her.

He was really good at this seduction game.

Enjoy an excerpt from

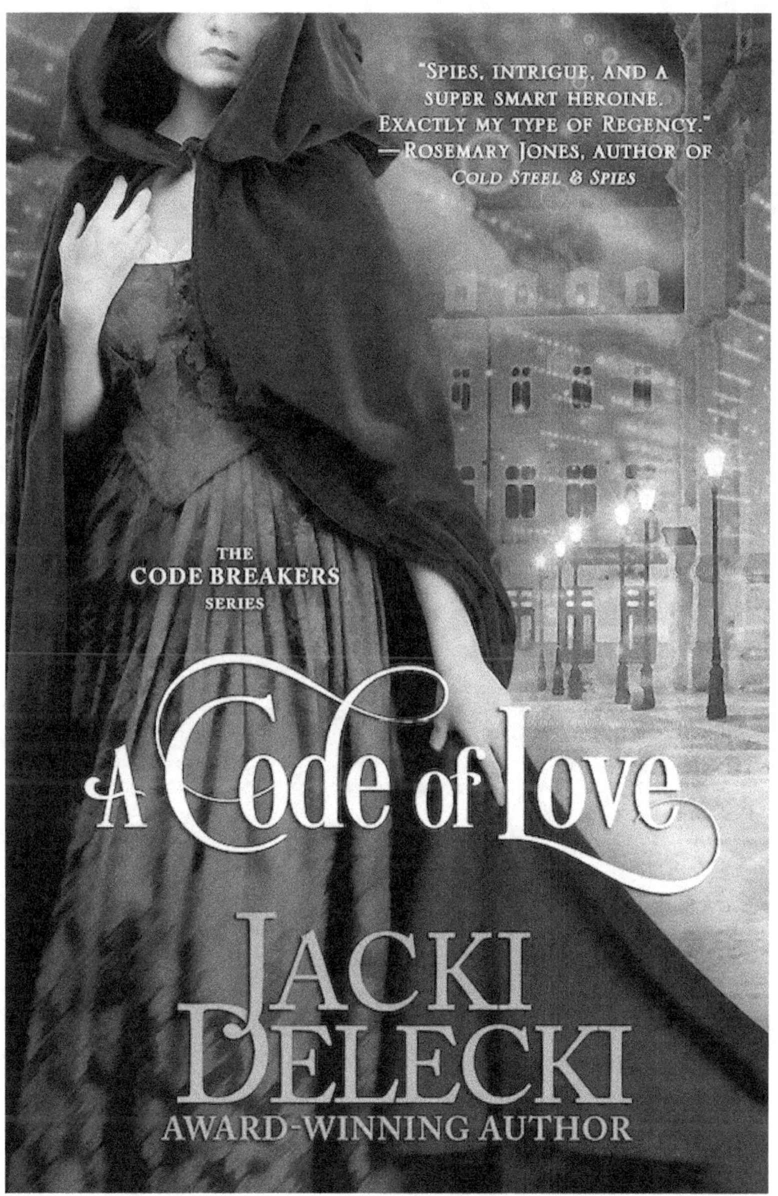
"SPIES, INTRIGUE, AND A
SUPER SMART HEROINE.
EXACTLY MY TYPE OF REGENCY."
—ROSEMARY JONES, AUTHOR OF
COLD STEEL & SPIES

THE
CODE BREAKERS
SERIES

A Code of Love

JACKI
DELECKI
AWARD-WINNING AUTHOR

PROLOGUE

1802, Paris

Lord Michael Ormond Harcourt crept along the darkened passageway. He had earned his reputation as a brilliant code breaker, but never before had he ventured into the realm of housebreaker. Henrietta was going to be furious not to be part of tonight's exciting intrigue.

He strained to listen for the sounds of the house in the wee hours of the morning. He heard nothing but his heartbeat pounding in his ears. Reassured he was the only one about, he allowed himself to release the breath he had been holding since he sneaked into Gaston Le Chiffre's house. He moved down the narrow corridor to his French colleague's office.

He had only been in Paris a fortnight when he developed suspicions about Gaston—a series of sensations, hushed silences when he walked into a room, the papers on his desk seeming to have been moved, and the persistent feeling he was being followed.

The final impetus to search Gaston's office came yesterday with the arrival of an anonymous note: "Something's afoot."

He gingerly opened the office door, inspecting the darkened corners before he entered. The dying fire cast shadows on the book-lined walls. A log shifted. The small crash startled him, causing his heart to thump against his chest.

He closed the door and moved to the center of the room, lit a taper, and placed it in the holder on the desk, then shuffled through the neat stacks of papers. He opened drawers, searching the contents.

He ran his hand across the smooth mahogany surface of the desk then passed his fingers along the rough underside. There he found a slightly recessed area in the far corner. His fingers

returned to the uneven surface. Applying pressure, there was a sudden give, followed by a compartment popping open on the top of the desk.

The secret compartment contained a leather book. He scanned the room before he removed the worn volume. He had never seen a code quite like this one: French scrawl preceded by endless rows of numbers. This French puzzle was better than a wrapped Christmas present. He stuffed the incredible find into his waistband. He would crack the code in the safety of his room, then return the book to its hiding place, all before Gaston awoke.

He blew out the taper and left the office. He backtracked through Gaston's garden. Carefully closing the garden gate, he entered the alley. The mixture of fog and smoke from the city's coal fires blanketed the city. He could see no more than a few feet ahead. The cloying darkness muffled the distant voices, the clatter of carriage wheels, and horses' hooves.

Approaching the street, he slowed his pace. Hanging lanterns illuminated the walkway where he emerged from the unlit alley.

He turned and walked toward his house. In the thick fog, the sound of his footsteps resonated, booming with each step.

The hairs on his neck prickled when he heard another set of footsteps shuffling behind him. With only a few yards to reach home, he ran, never pausing to look back.

With his right hand, he reached into his greatcoat for his pistol; with his left, he lunged for the doorknob.

The report of a pistol echoed down the street. An intense heat penetrated his awareness. He stumbled forward.

The door opened from the inside. The lights around Denby, his manservant, gave him an angelic halo.

"Close the door, man."

"My lord, what is it?"

"I've been shot." The room grew dimmer. "Get this book to Hen."

BOOKS BY JACKI DELECKI

Romantic Suspense:

GRAYCE WALTERS SERIES
An Inner Fire
Women Under Fire
Men Under Fire
Marriage Under Fire

Historical Romantic Suspense

THE CODE BREAKER SERIES
A Code of Love
A Christmas Code
A Code of the Heart

ABOUT THE AUTHOR

Jacki Delecki is a Best-Selling, Romantic Suspense writer. Delecki's **Grayce Walters Series**, which chronicles the adventures of a Seattle animal acupuncturist, was an editor's selection by USA Today. Delecki's Romantic Regency **The Code Breaker Series** hit number one on Amazon. Both acclaimed series are available for purchase at http://www.JackiDelecki.com.

To learn more about Jacki and her books and to be the first to hear about giveaways join her newsletter found on her website. Follow her on FB–Jacki Delecki; Twitter @jackidelecki.

www.ingramcontent.com/pod-product-compliance
Lightning Source LLC
Chambersburg PA
CBHW072145130726
47909CB00004BB/1220